FIVE GRAVES TO BOOT HILL

Four Rangers had been gunned down. But Terrell, a Ranger with a reputation, swore vengeance on the killers. Soon he was behind enemy lines . . . just another member of the gang . . . and he would have to force their hand . . . their gun hands!

GORDON D. SHIRREFFS

FIVE GRAVES TO BOOT HILL

Complete and Unabridged

LINFORD
Leicester

SHI
LARGE
PRINT

First published in the USA in 1968 by
Tower Publications, Inc.,
New York

First Linford Edition
published August 1987

British Library CIP Data

Shirreffs, Gordon D.
  Five graves to Boot Hill.—Large print ed.—
Linford western library
I. Title
813'.54[F]   PS3569.H562

ISBN 0-7089-6411-7

Published by
F. A. Thorpe (Publishing) Ltd.
Anstey, Leicestershire
Set by Rowland Phototypesetting Ltd.
Bury St. Edmunds, Suffolk
Printed and bound in Great Britain by
T. J. Press (Padstow) Ltd., Padstow, Cornwall

1

THE West Texas rain was driving full into the lean face of the rider on the El Paso Road. It glistened from his yellow slicker as lightning flashed across the streaming skies and illuminated in ghastly light the wet desert between the Rimrocks and the Rio Grande. Somewhere up ahead was the tiny *placita* of Aguila, hardly more than a wide spot in the road, and thirty miles from Ysleta. A man was waiting there for Buck Terrell. Buck did not know him by sight, but knew him very well by reputation.

The lightning flashed eerily across the foothills and flickered along the serrated crests of the mountains, a lonely and forbidding sight to most men, but to Buck Terrell there was something in it that was home. A man's birthplace is etched in his heart, both the good and the bad of it. Buck had been West Texas born, and away from the land of his birth too long. It had not been wholly his choice, for a man does not

1

know the winding trail into the future. Perhaps it is just as well.

The thought was Buck's as he turned his body away from the searching wind and the chilling rain to shape a cigarette, shielding it in a big brown hand as he lighted it. He drew in the satisfying smoke as he turned again to face the wind. As he did so he felt the paper in his shirt pocket rub against his chest. That piece of paper had brought him all the way from Laredo, about five hundred miles away as the crow flies and a bit longer by road, back to the windy wastes of West Texas. It had brought him through the cold, rainy night, forcing on an already tired horse, while Buck himself was long saddle weary and in urgent need of a bath and a good night's sleep. By stagecoach, train and horseback he had come, and even now, after so many miles and so many monotonous days he did not know why he had been ordered to go to Aguila and to be there on a specific date. That date was this very day, or what was left of it.

The country was now plunged in the wet darkness. Not a light showed its friendly yellow pinpoint on either side of the road or up ahead, and he knew without turning in his wet saddle that there was none behind him either. It was almost as though Buck had ridden clear off the face of the earth and was wandering in some uninhabited void somewhere between the earth and the other spinning planets. Now and then he would look back when the sheet lightning would etch itself against the skies, half expecting to see someone riding far behind him, yet not trying to overtake him. He had had that uneasy feeling in the back of his mind ever since he had left lonely Sierra Blanca. The road was almost always empty, as it had been for the past thirty miles, except during the day he had occasionally seen a wagon and team or at times a foot-plodding Mexican driving a laden burro ahead of him, although once an oncoming horseman had turned hard off the road ahead of him and had ridden swiftly out of sight. It was nothing unusual in the empty land of West Texas.

When he did see a pinpoint of light ahead of him he was almost startled. The lights stood out in the darkness like the yellow eyes of a pair of cougars waiting there on the road for an unwary traveler. He let the horse plod on; there was no use in hurrying him now. The dun had done his job for that day.

Buck swung down from the saddle as he reached the first adobe house of Aguila. It was sagging and uncared for, its clay walls soaked with the steady rains and with water streaming into the muddy street from crude wooden rain spouts. Not a soul was to be seen on the one street of the little *poblado*, although the street was actually the road itself, which continued on into the darkness as though it had far more important business to the west. Buck led the dun beneath a dripping ramada shelter that sagged next to an abandoned adobe. Buck shaped another cigarette and lighted it under the shelter of the *ramada* and then he unbuttoned his worn slicker and slid his right hand down to touch his sheathed six-gun, low slung and tied down. His left hand felt the cold metal of a double-barreled derringer in his coat pocket. He grinned in the darkness. "Formally attired for an evening walk in Aguila," he said.

He tethered his horse and then walked out into the rain, heading toward the biggest adobe in town. It was easy enough to see in the flashes of lightning. It was better built and better cared for than any of the others, and had apparently been recently plastered. Perhaps it was the *casa* of the *alcalde*, doubling as the local cantina.

Even Aguila would have such an official as an *alcalde*, the mayor. Straggling along the road and on either side of it were a number of other adobes and *jacales*. There was a sway-backed warehouse, several peeled-pole corrals and the ruins of the old Butterfield & Company stage-coach swing station.

Buck squelched through the thick pasty mud to the largest adobe and stopped in front of the big wooden, bolt-studded door. He looked up and down the street. Not a soul in sight. He boot toed the door three times and then waited. A trickle of icy water worked down inside his slicker collar. He cursed softly as he waited. It was almost like a "blue norther" that wild and wet night. He booted the door again. It opened a hairline crack. There was someone just behind the door peering out at Buck. "Well?" demanded Buck. "You aim to keep me out here all night?"

"What is it you want, *señor*?" asked a Mexican.

"Food and shelter for the night, *amigo*," answered Buck.

"It is very late."

"I know that!" snapped Buck. "That's just why I want in!"

5

The Mexican hesitated, then allowed the heavy door to creak back on its great hinges. Buck pushed past him into the rather narrow hallway. It reeked of close bad air, a commingling of whiskey slops, greasy food, the stale odor of long unwashed clothing and hanging through it, like a pungent thread woven into the close fabric, was the ever-present smell of horses. One never got far from such an odor in West Texas. Buck peeled off his dripping slicker and let the little Mexican pass by him toward the door of the common room of the place. The door was closed and as the Mexican opened it a flood of smoky yellow light mingled with woodsmoke flowed into the darker hallway. The Mexican quickly stepped aside as the door banged against the wall, letting Buck stand there in the full light of the common room. Buck cursed mentally. Any man in that room, behind the flare of light, had Buck mercilessly exposed while he himself was protected by the light that half blinded Buck coming from the semi-darkness of the hallway. Buck walked quickly inside, bumping against a heavy chair, while the Mexican catfooted in behind him.

The big, smoky room was empty of human life other than Buck and the Mexican. The

Mexican had walked behind a high, zinc-topped bar and was studying Buck closely with liquid brown eyes. Buck caught the odor of tobacco smoke as he took off his hat and slashed it sideways to free it of the rainwater. "You surely smoke up a storm all by yourself," observed Buck. He walked to the end of the bar and placed his back against the thick and scabrous wall.

"Your pleasure, *señor*?" said the Mexican mechanically.

"Beer will do tonight," said Buck.

It was then that the eerie feeling came over Buck that he was being watched. There was nothing that really warned him, except that sixth sense of the man who lives on the raw edge of danger and violence, and God knew Buck had done that long enough to have this sense hand-honed and mirror polished. Buck shaped another cigarette. The windows were all closed and shuttered. Likely they hadn't been opened in twenty years. There were two doors at the far end of the room beyond the big beehive fireplace. One of the doors was tightly closed while the other was ajar.

The beer-bottle cap popped up as the binding wire was pulled free and the foaming brew

7

flowed over the neck of the brown bottle. "Glass?" asked the Mexican.

"Bottle," said Buck as he lighted his cigarette, peering over the flare of the match toward that slightly ajar door.

"You have come a long way, *señor?*" asked the Mexican.

"Perhaps," said Buck.

"From Marfa, perhaps?"

Buck sipped at the beer. It was good and cold. "Perhaps," he said through the foam. He wiped his lips with the back of his right hand, holding the bottle with his left, ready for a draw if something broke loose. He was still being watched. He sipped at the beer again and looked right into the Mexican's brown eyes with a hard look from his cold gray eyes. "You can tell that nosey hombre behind that door that he can come out into the open, mister," he said. "That is, if he wants to look me in the eye man to man. I don't like Peeping Toms one little bit."

The bartender began to polish a glass with the corner of a soiled towel. He carefully placed the glass atop a pyramid of other glasses. "Perhaps you have come from Laredo," he said over his shoulder.

Buck looked at the back of the man's head, keeping a back bar mirror reflection of that door in his eyes. "Perhaps I just might have come from Laredo," he said.

"Terrell?" a quiet voice said.

Buck turned quickly, placing the beer bottle on the zinc while his right hand dropped toward the worn walnut butt of his Colt. A rather slightly built man was standing in the doorway that led to the hallway. There was a faint smile on his lean brown face. "You've changed in the last ten years, Buck," he said.

Buck's eyes narrowed, and then a swift smile of recognition broke out on his face. "Sergeant Lynch!" he said.

Lynch walked forward, limping slightly. "Captain Lynch now, Terrell," he said, extending his hand. "Don't mind Chico there behind the bar. He's one of the best friends the Texas Rangers have ever had. That's why I arranged to meet you here. It took me a few minutes to recognize you, although I must admit you had me fooled for a time. You have changed, even you must admit, from that long-legged, gangling kid in El Paso years past."

Buck gripped the officer's hand. Buck's left hand touched the disfiguring scar on his left cheek. "This, and the mustache, plus ten years, *have* changed me," he admitted.

"That's the very reason I asked to have you transferred west into the Frontier Battalion. That, and the fact that you know this West Texas country as well as any man I know. No one knows, of course, that you *have* been transferred out here?"

"No one but Headquarters and my company commander."

"*Bueno!* Chico, put some bottles of cold beer on a tray, bring some chile and plenty of tortillas for Mister Terrell. Anything else, Buck?" said the officer.

"My dun is still out in the wet, captain."

Chico smiled. "I, myself, will go and get him. He has come a long way and deserves the very best. There is a fine dry stable behind this *casa*. Do not worry about the *caballo*, *Señor* Terrell."

"He's down at the end *jacal*, under the ramada."

Buck followed Captain Lynch into another room. In a few minutes Chico brought in a big bowl of steaming, succulent chile and beans, along with a plate of warm tortillas. Captain Lynch paced back and forth, with a cigar

10

clenched between his teeth, as Buck ate. "Only sheer desperation would force me to request that a Ranger be transferred all the way from Laredo out here to the Frontier Battalion, Buck. We had to have a man who knew this country well, yet was comparatively unknown as a Ranger—locally in any case. A man with plenty of guts, a fast gun and willing to work under cover."

Buck's chile-filled tortilla stopped in mid-air between bowl and mouth. He tilted his head to one side. "*Undercover?*" he quietly asked.

"Exactly!"

"I work *behind* the star, sir. I like it that way, sir."

Lynch waved an impatient hand. "Of course you do! We all do!" he said sharply. "No real man likes spying, undercover work, peeking and prying and all that goes with it. Like you, I'd rather walk into a fight, wearing the star, than have to sneak around like a coyote in the dark. But the situation is desperate out here, Terrell! Let me tell you, it took some time for us to place our finger on just the right man for this job. You're tailor-made for it, Buck."

Buck finished off the chile-loaded tortilla and

filled another. "They might have consulted me first," he said a little bitterly.

"It was a question of picking just the right man. You filled the specifications."

Buck munched on the rich food and finished it off. He wiped his chin with the back of a hand and felt for the makings. "It just beats the hell out of me why Texas Rangers have to work this way, Captain Lynch. It just isn't my way, sir."

"Nor mine!" snapped Lynch. "I can't say I exactly like your attitude, Terrell!"

Buck snapped a match on his thumbnail and lit the cigarette, eyeing Lynch over the flare of the match. "Unfortunately," he murmured, "the Regulations prevent me from answering the way I feel."

Lynch picked up a chair, twirled it around, then dropped into it, resting his folded arms on the back of it to study Buck. "Forget the Regulations and the difference in rank, Buck," he said quietly. "I want you to know that I don't want you to take on this assignment except on a purely voluntary basis."

Buck blew a smoke ring and poked a finger through it. "That's not the way your letter to Headquarters put it. I was simply transferred out here. Actually I had been trying to get a transfer out to the Frontier Battalion for quite some time."

"I knew that too," said Lynch with a winning grin.

Buck smiled crookedly. "So you thought you'd kill two birds with one stone, eh, captain?"

"Say rather a number of outlaws with one Texas Ranger," said Lynch enigmatically.

Buck emptied his beer bottle and opened another one. "I ought to get stinking drunk," he said morosely, "but it will take more than this beer to do the right job." He looked up at Lynch. "It's a helluva long way for a man to come to do a dirty undercover job."

"I said it was voluntary," said the officer. His keen blue eyes studied Buck. "You see, Buck, it was through your company commander at Laredo, the officials at Headquarters, and yours truly, Dan Lynch, that we took a long chance on having you transferred out here without knowledge of what we expected of you, and still believing you wouldn't let us down."

"You might as well fill me in on the details," said Buck. He cocked his head to listen to the steady drumming of the cold rain on the flat roof of the big *casa*. "I don't aim to go anywhere on a night like this."

Lynch felt inside his coat and brought out a silver cigar case. "Get rid of that quirly and try one of these long nines," he suggested. "It will be quite a story, Buck."

Buck selected a long nine and bit the end from it. He held the tip over the lip of the Argand lamp cylinder and drew fiery life into the good weed. He blew out a cloud of smoke and shifted in his seat. His rump still ached from the miles of long, hard riding, and all for nothing, as it had turned out.

Lynch lit a cigar and sat there thoughtfully for a moment, looking at the scabrous plaster of the wall as though he was seeing right through it, out into the rain drenched night, and miles and miles beyond that. "I recall you were seventeen years old when you left West Texas and enlisted in the Army. You got that beauty mark on your face when a Lipan tried to take off your head with a honed butcher knife in that bitch of a brawl near Cibolo. After that you were transferred to Fort Riley, up in Kansas, until your hitch was up. After that you rode range in Oklahoma, did some mining in Colorado, tried ranching for a time in Central

14

Texas, then enlisted in the Texas Rangers three years ago, which, if you don't mind me saying, was what the hell you should have done in the first place!"

"*Gracias*," said Buck dryly.

"*Por nada*," said Dan Lynch. "Since leaving West Texas," he continued, "you've gained twenty pounds and not an ounce of it is fat. You acquired that beautiful scar and that hecoon of a mustache. All of this, plus the passage of ten years' time, has changed you quite considerably from the rawboned kid who left this country to make a hero out of himself riding with the yellowlegs."

"Go on," said Buck. "You haven't missed much."

"Including a fine-toothed going over of your Ranger record," said Lynch. He blew a smoke puff to accentuate his remark.

"I've only done my job," said Buck.

"They say you're a dedicated man, Buck."

Buck inspected his cigar as though he had never seen one before. "I took the oath as a Texas Ranger," he said simply. "I meant every word of it."

"Exactly," said Dan. He sipped at his beer. "Do you still feel the same way?"

"This trip hasn't changed me any, if that's what you mean."

Lynch speared him with those penetrating blue eyes of his. "How do you feel about Texas Rangers getting killed in the line of duty?"

Buck shrugged. "It's part of the game. Why do you ask?"

Lynch leaned forward. "I don't mean in man-to-man fighting, Buck. Like walking through gunsmoke to meet the chunk of lead that was fashioned for your guts by the hand of fate. I mean like getting shot down like an ox is felled by the mallet in a slaughterhouse, never knowing what killed him." His voice rose a little. "I mean that Texas Rangers have been murdered out here in the line of duty. Not killed in man-to-man gunplay or anything like that, but *murdered* in cold blood! Now, just how do you feel about *that*, Mister Buck Terrell?"

Buck looked into those hard blue eyes. "You know the unwritten law as well as I do," he said quietly. "Track 'em down if it takes being twenty-four hours in the saddle. Keep going until you find the killer or killers, then save the sovereign State of Texas the cost of a trial and an execution."

16

"We've lost too many Rangers that way out here, Buck, and not one of them has been avenged, nor have any of the killers ever been brought into custody and to justice."

"It doesn't say much for the Frontier Battalion," said Buck sarcastically.

"They said you were a hard man, Terrell."

"I do my job," said Buck levelly.

Their eyes seemed to clash, then Dan Lynch looked down to re-light his cigar. "Somewhere in the area around here, north to the New Mexico line, and south-easterly past, and including the Big Bend country, there ride the men who have killed Texas Rangers. We can't get a real lead on them, Buck. We have nothing but powerful suspicions. There isn't one real fact upon which to hang a charge upon any of them! Nothing except the knowledge that Ranger killers are still on the loose, breaking the law, killing people, including our comrades in the Rangers, in cold blood."

Buck looked up. "How many Rangers, Captain Lynch?"

Lynch did not answer right away. He reached inside his coat and withdrew a faded manila envelope. From it he shook out four photographs that dropped within the soft yellow pool of light from the shaded lamp. Lynch aligned the photographs in a certain order. Buck looked into the strong faces beneath the wide-brimmed hats. The lean, wind- and sun-lined faces of the steady-eyed men who had ridden proudly behind the star. He studied them and then his eyes suddenly narrowed. He placed a finger on the end photograph and then looked slowly up into the face of the Ranger captain. "This one," he asked softly. "Who is he?"

Dan Lynch raised his head a little. "When was the last time you were home, Buck?" he asked.

"Six years ago. For my mother's funeral."

Lynch looked down at the picture. "Take another look," he invited. "A close look, Buck."

Buck passed a big brown hand across his face. "That man is my kid-brother Frank," he said slowly.

"That's right," said Dan. "He enlisted a year ago as soon as he was old enough. He knew you were one of the best Texas Rangers in the Laredo area and he wanted to make a name for himself with the Frontier Battalion before he told you he was in the Rangers. He was killed, *murdered* I should say, on his first scout into the Big Bend country."

A fly buzzed sluggishly around the beer slops on the table and then crawled on the end photograph leaving a faint trail of filth across the fresh young face of Frank Terrell. Buck swept the fly to one side and wiped the photograph clean with his scarf. "He was only a kid," he said softly, as though to himself. "I was sending him money hoping he'd go to school and get a decent education, like my father had. I wanted him to be somebody! I wanted him to be a businessman, or a lawyer or a doctor, but I wanted him to be *somebody*. . . ."

"He *was* somebody," said Lynch quietly. "He was a Texas Ranger."

Buck placed the photograph in line with the others. "When do I start?" he asked simply.

Lynch smiled. He placed a hand on Buck's shoulder. "God help me, Buck, but it went against the grain to have to do it this way."

Buck shook his head. "Forget it. You needed a Ranger for a particular job. Had I known Frank and the others I would have demanded a transfer out here, and if I hadn't received it, I would have resigned to come west to do the job on my own."

19

"We figured that out," said the officer. "Fate has curious ways of working things out. But, it's a cruel thing for you, Buck."

Buck looked up at him. It seemed to Dan Lynch that Buck Terrell had changed even more in the past few minutes. "Forget it!" he snapped harshly. "What's the job? When do I start?"

Lynch got up and walked to the door. He left the room and was gone a few minutes. "Chico has closed tight for the night," he said when he returned. He placed a bucket of iced beer bottles on the floor. "We're alone in the place. Your dun has been taken care of. I've got to leave here long before dawn and be on my way back to Ysleta. I don't want to be seen around Aguila, nor in your company at this time, Buck."

"Go on," said Buck as he fished out two bottles and popped them open. "It looks like a long night."

"Chico has been working for us for some years. His cousin, Francisco Armenderiz, was a Ranger in the Frontier Battalion." Lynch placed a finger on the first of the four photographs. "This is Francisco—one of the best men we ever had. He was a handsome man, as

20

you can see. But he was hardly recognizable when we found his body near Maravillas Creek in the Big Bend. Since that time Chico has sworn to help us run down his killers. This has been to our advantage. One of the men whom we suspect either had something to do with the killings, or is mixed up with those who did, is due here tomorrow night on his way back from El Paso to Fort Davis, or so we believe.

"This man has power in the Big Bend country. We've never been able to pin anything on him. We've tried time and time again to slip an undercover man into his *corrida*, but with no luck." Lynch placed a finger on the second photograph. "This is, or was, Cooke Durkee, one of the best veterans in the battalion. Cooke took a long chance on not being recognized. He had served most of the time along the New Mexican border. We found him a month after he had been hung to a tree near Tornillo Draw." Lynch paused and looked steadily at Buck. "The only way we could identify him was by a curious bullet scar on his left thigh. The crows and *zopilotes* had taken care of his upper body. It was one helluva gruesome sight."

21

"Hanging?" asked Buck incredulously. "Hanging a Texas Ranger?"

Lynch nodded. "The third man here is Kelly Ledbetter."

Buck's head snapped up. "Kelly Ledbetter? I can't believe it!"

"Kelly was a legend in the Frontier Battalion. He was too well known to work undercover but he had more guts and gall than a brass monkey. Kelly was a real Ranger, Buck. One of the best."

"The best," said Buck. "He saved my life in the Army in that Donnybrook at Cibolo." He touched the scar on his face. "Kelly was the best friend a man could have had." He looked more intently at the third picture, for in his shock at recognizing his own brother he had not studied the three other pictures too closely. It had been years since he had seen Kelly, and in the early days Kelly had not been sporting that magnificent dragoon mustache he affected in the faded photograph. Now he recognized in the man the face of the boy who had been his youthful friend and who had ridden stirrup-to-stirrup with him in the yellowlegs.

"Do you want to know what they did to Kelly?" asked Dan quietly.

22

"Don't leave out anything," said Buck.

"From the looks of things they had caught him unawares. They had stripped him and driven him through the tornillo brush and catclaw until his hide must have been ribboned and slashed by the cruel needles and thorns. They looped a horsehair *reata* about his neck and pulled him behind a running horse until he fell and then he was dragged over the cruel ground on a talus slope of razor-edge rock until even his own Maker would have failed to recognize him, Buck! They left his poor corpse in the center of the road near Terlingua Creek with a tin star shaped roughly like that of a Texas Ranger stuck into his naked chest with a Mexican *cuchillo*."

Buck stared in disbelief at the officer. "And you have no idea who did all this?"

"That's why we sent for you, Buck."

"Who is the man who is due here tomorrow night?"

"Name of Powers Rorkin. As I said—we have nothing on him. We must get a man into his confidence, or at least into a position to join his *corrida*, for we're almost sure he is the leader of an outlaw *corrida* of the toughest boots and hard cases in the Big Bend country."

"He sounds cagey," said Buck thoughtfully. "How do you propose getting me into his confidence?"

"You'll do the job then?" asked the officer.

Buck looked down at the four pictures. Four dead men. Four *murdered* men. One of them his brother and one of them his best friend of years past. Four good men who had obviously died the hard way without a chance to put up a fight. "Is there any further question about it?" he asked quietly.

Lynch smiled. "Have another long nine, Buck. I'm leaving here in exactly one hour, and before I leave here, there is a great deal you must learn and memorize."

The icy rain slashed against the walls and roof of the big *cantina*, and the distant thunder growled throatily in the mountain gorges to the north, while Captain Dan Lynch spun out a plan with all the skill and patience of a spider.

2

THE rain had stopped before the dawn of the new day, with Dan Lynch long gone from Aguila. A cold wind had swept down from the mountains with the coming of the dawn, chilling both man and beast caught in the unprotected open. Buck Terrell rode into Aguila an hour after dusk and tethered his dun in front of Chico's *cantina*. He had spent a miserable day hiding out in a rain soaked draw northwest of the *placita* where he could watch passersby on the road, smoking innumerable cigarettes and nipping occasionally at a bottle of good aguardiente given to him by Chico.

He walked through the long and narrow hallway to the door of the big barroom and paused a moment in the doorway. The heat flowed about his chilled body as he stood there, quickly scanning the occupants of the barroom. He walked behind the one man who stood at the bar, shielded by a huge Mexican hat. He glanced casually at Buck as Buck reached the end of the bar and turned to place his back against the wall, as he had done the night before while waiting to be contacted by Dan Lynch. The man at the bar emptied his beer glass and then held the empty bottle above it, slapping the base of it as though to coax the last drops from it. "Bartender!" he cried. "Beer!"

Buck looked away from him. He was a Texas Ranger plant. Chico served the man and came down to Buck. "Your pleasure, *señor?*" he asked.

"Aguardiente," said Buck. He looked into the cracked, fly-specked mirror behind the bar and saw a man seated at a table in a far corner of the big room, with a chile bowl and coffee cup shoved to one side, while he read a newspaper. Buck knew well enough that he was not quite as interested in the newspaper as he was in the newcomer who stood at the end of the bar. There was another man seated at a table near the end of the bar. His upper body was stretched out on the dirty table top, his face resting in the liquor slops, while he clutched an empty tequila bottle in one hand and an empty shot glass in the other. A sluggish fly buzzed curiously about his gaping mouth.

Buck sipped the aguardiente. "How far to El Paso?" he asked Chico.

"Perhaps thirty-five miles," said Chico. "There are rooms here, *señor*. Cheap and clean. There is breakfast in the morning."

Buck refilled his glass. "I'll think about it," he said. He grinned. "Any girls?"

Chico nodded. "I can arrange it later on. Young. Pretty. Willing. How about it?"

Buck shook his head ruefully. "Can't even afford a *puta*," he said. "Helluva note, ain't it?"

Minutes ticked slowly past. It was quiet in the barroom except for the occasional clinking of glass against glass, the gentle snoring of the drunk and all of it overlaid by the faint moaning of the wind about the walls of the *cantina*.

The outer door of the *cantina* banged against the wall. It slammed shut. Boots scuffled grittily along the passageway to the door of the barroom. Buck slewed his eyes sideways to look at the wall clock. Seven o'clock. He drained his glass and shoved it back, turning a little toward the doorway. A tall, broad-shouldered man was suddenly framed in the doorway. Lawman seemed to be stamped all over his face. Buck lowered his hand toward his Colt. He glanced toward a rear door.

27

"Wait a minute, Spade!" said the man in the doorway. "Don't you make no break!"

Buck turned a little, with his hand resting on his Colt butt.

"You can't run forever, Spade," said the man in the doorway.

"I aim to keep on runnin', Langford," he said in a low voice. "Don't you try to stop me."

The man between Buck and Langford hastily stepped away from the bar. Chico wet his full lips and crouched a little as though ready to drop behind the bar. The drunk snored on. The man at the other table slowly lowered his newspaper.

Langford held out a big hand. "Don't you draw on me, Spade," he warned. "You can't get away this time. I've already wired ahead to El Paso. They'll be waiting for you there. You get north again into New Mexico and you know it as well as I do. *Take your hand off that gun, Spade!*"

Buck glanced about like a cornered rat then went into a crouch, whipping up his Colt, thumbing back the hammer and stabbing the six-gun toward Langford. Langford cursed and jumped to one side, clawing down with his right hand for a draw. Buck's Colt spat flame and

28

smoke. Langford jerked spasmodically, staring unbelievingly at the man he called Spade, then he slapped his left hand hard against his broad chest and ripped aside his coat as though to reach his flesh. Blood spread swiftly in an ugly, irregular stain across his shirt. He tried to reach his Colt, swayed back and forth, then drew the Colt. It clattered onto the floor from nerveless fingers. Langford took three faltering steps forward. His mouth was squared. "I . . . I . . . I . . ." he said. That was as far as he got. He fell sideways against a table. Bottles and glasses crashed to the floor. Langford lay still for a moment and then his clawed right hand crept across the filth of the floor and closed tightly.

Gunsmoke rifted through the room. Buck's lips had drawn back from his teeth like the snarl of a lobo. The scar on his left cheek stood out like a thick worm trying to force its way through the tanned skin. "Anyone else want to try to stop Spade Cleburne?" he asked softly. He grinned crookedly. His cocked Colt was steady in his hand at waist level, finger tip on trigger, and a promise of sudden and violent death in the icy eyes.

"Mother of God," said Chico as he stood up from behind the bar. "What shall I do?"

The man in the Mexican hat walked to the bar, emptied his beer bottle into his gullet and then lowered it. He wiped his mouth both ways with the back of his left hand. "If I was you, *amigo*, I'd damned soon get rid of that corpse. Such a thing could put a noose around all of our necks."

The drunk had been aroused by the single shot. He stared stupidly at the dead man and then at Buck. "Jesus God," he said thickly. "A man can't even get in a good drunk's sleep around here no more without all hell breakin' loose."

Chico rounded the end of the bar and stepped gingerly over the dead man's legs. He ran out of the barroom and dropped the bars across the outer door, then came swiftly back into the quiet barroom. His face was set and white and dewed with cold sweat. He crossed himself. "*Madre de Dios*," he said. "I don't want trouble." He gripped the drunk by the shoulder. "Give me a hand, *amigo*."

The man in the big Mex hat nodded. "We work together or we might hang together." He gripped Langford under the arms, and with the help of Chico and the drunk, the heavy body

30

was carried into the passageway and through it to a back door.

Buck had not moved, but now his eyes swiveled toward the man at the table. "And what about you, mister?" he quietly asked.

The man folded his newspaper. He got up and walked to the bar. He filled a glass with aguardiente and shoved it toward Buck. "If I was you, hombre," he said quietly, "I'd cut stick for the Rio Grande."

Buck took the proffered glass and quickly downed the potent brandy. He wiped his mouth with the back of a dirty hand. "To hell with them!" he snarled. "I'm not runnin' anymore! Let them come on, one at a time or all together! I can handle them!"

The man smiled. "Much brandy is the drink for heroes," he said. "I can smell the blood and guts already. Chico won't talk, and you can see how those other two reacted."

Buck held the man with his eyes. "And you?" he questioned.

The man shrugged. "I've got no love for the law, mister. You down on your luck and on the run?"

"Look at me," said Buck.

The man looked down at the dirty, cracked

boots with the badly runover heels, the worn levis, the threadbare shirt and worn jacket. He didn't know it, but the costume, with odor attached, had been given to Buck before he had left Aguila to hide out in the draw. Every sign denoted saddle tramp, bum and drifter. But, the Colt was clean and the drifter knew how to use it. It was the hard eyes that held the man, however. "I'm Powers Rorkin," he said. His hard green eyes flicked a glance toward Buck. "You know me?"

"Can't say I do," said Buck.

"You know *of* me?"

Buck grinned a little. "Somewhat," he admitted. Rorkin was a taller man than Buck, but not as solid and muscular through the chest and shoulders. His Mexican dandy mustache was neatly trimmed, and waxed. Few Texans cared, or dared, to wax their mustaches. They left such affectations to dudes, dandies and gamblers, and *bravo* Mexicans who wore such mustaches almost as a trademark. Rorkin's lips were a little too full for his lean face; they were almost loose and sensual, but there was nothing else *loose* about this man. Buck could almost smell death emanating from his presence.

"You shoot fast, mister," said Powers Rorkin

as he filled up Buck's glass and then one for himself.

"I learned the hard way, Mister Rorkin."

"Texas man by your speech."

Buck grinned. "Who else can shoot like that?"

Rorkin jerked his head toward the back of the big room. "Who was he?" he asked.

"Langford? Deputy United States Marshal. The bastard tailed me all the way from Oklahoma Territory."

The hard green eyes flickered a little. "United States Marshal? You play a hard game, Cleburne. You loco or something?"

Buck's face was a mask of hell and hate. "You figure I *wanted* to go back there? They'd have hung me for sure."

Rorkin waved a hand. "All the same, mister. That was a *Federal* agent. Mother of God, as Chico always says! You play a wild game, Cleburne."

Buck flipped open the loading gate of the Colt and then ejected the empty brass hull. It tinkled on the floor. He fished a fresh round from his gunbelt and reloaded the empty chamber but his eyes never left those of Rorkin. He snapped shut the loading gate, twirled the heavy weapon on a forefinger, then slid it easily into its shaped holster. "Like you said: Chico and the other two won't talk. What about you?" he asked.

"I advised you to cut stick for the Rio Grande, didn't I? Watch out for the Rurales on the Mex side of the Rio. They've been working hand-in-glove with the Texas Rangers lately."

Buck shoved back his battered hat. "Christ's Blood," he said thoughtfully. "They're waiting for me down El Paso way. I can't make it to the New Mexican border, and even if I did the New Mexico lawmen are looking for me as well as the Texas Rangers. If I get across the river the Rurales will be looking for me. I'm damned if I run and damned if I don't, Mister Rorkin."

Rorkin thoughtfully bit off the end of a cigar and lighted the weed. "There's always use for a fast gun in certain places," he said casually.

"Such as?"

The green eyes looked through the wreathing tobacco smoke. "I'm heading southwest myself," said Rorkin. "I planned to stay here this night, but not now. I want no trouble around here. Beyond Esperanza we can head into the Quitman Mountains and then cut past the Eagles toward the Van Horns. After that, no lawman will be able to track us."

"You want me to go along then? To where?"

Rorkin rubbed his lean jaw. "What difference does it make to you now, Cleburne? You're just a spit and a jump ahead of the law right now. It's either ride with me or be taken back to Oklahoma Territory for a dance at the end of a rope. I'm leaving. You can come along, or do what you will." He emptied his glass and walked toward the door. He passed into the hallway and a moment later Buck heard Rorkin remove the bars from the outer door. Then the door slammed shut behind the outlaw.

Chico came into the barroom. "OK?" he asked.

Buck nodded. "It worked like a charm. It looks like a long, cold ride to the southwest through the Quitmans, past the Eagles and then toward the Van Horns. That's all I know. Is everything under control, *amigo?*"

Chico grinned. "The *corpse* will be well taken care of, *amigo*. Go with God, Señor Terrell." He reached under the bar and brought forth a bottle of aguardiente. "It will be a long, cold ride, as you have said. Take this to keep you warm."

Buck left the *cantina* and untethered the dun. He swung up into the saddle and spurred the dun toward the end of the single street. A dim form was moving off to the southwest. Powers Rorkin was heading for the Quitmans, as he had said he would. Buck looked back toward the *cantina*. It had been a good stroke of fortune that Rorkin hadn't looked too closely at the *corpse* of "Deputy United States Marshal Langford." Blanks don't leave bullet holes. Langford was actually Sergeant Mike Adams of the Texas Rangers, and not a member of the Frontier Battalion, nor was he known in West Texas. He had been sent from San Antonio to pick up a wanted man in El Paso for delivery in San Antonio. Captain Dan Lynch had drafted him to play the part of Deputy United States Marshal Langford. Langford was an accomplished actor. He had proved it by his appearance in the barroom and by his deft smashing of the thin walled glass vial of red dye he had carried in his shirt pocket. The man in the big Mexican hat was a new member of the Texas Rangers who had agreed to go along with the little but tense drama being played out in the barroom, while the besotted drunk was a cousin to Chico. Rorkin had been neatly taken in, as far as Buck could see, but if Rorkin suspected Buck, he would end up the same way

Armenderiz, Durkee, Ledbetter and his brother Frank had done—dead at the hand of a person, or persons unknown. *Then there would be five graves to Boot Hill instead of four*. Buck didn't intend to fill that yawning fifth grave, not, at least, until he had found the killers of the four Texas Rangers that had preceded him on his mission. It was a big chaw he had bitten off.

Langford's "resurrection" would take place far away from Aguila and by that time, Buck hoped he would be well established with Rorkin and his bloody handed *corrida*. Still, there was a thread of suspicion in the cautious and wary mind of Buck Terrell, not quite fitting itself into the warp and woof of his thought patterns. It had been easy, perhaps *too* easy, to carry off the trickery on Powers Rorkin. Not for one second could Buck let down his guard. One slight mistake might lead to a violent death.

Buck caught up with Rorkin. The outlaw glanced sideways at him, nodded, but did not speak. They rode steadily along the little-used road that trended ever southwest while the keening wind swept tumbleweeds across the road or worked loose spurts of drying grit to drive them hard against man and horse. Rorkin was a puzzler to Buck, as he had been to the

Frontier Battalion. Bible Number Two, the list of wanted criminals kept strictly up to date by Texas Rangers Headquarters, did not list a Powers Rorkin, though it did list a number of men who might quite well fit his description, but a similar description is not a conviction. The name meant nothing—Texas was still a state where a surprisingly high percentage of citizens had several names in their backgrounds.

They camped that night in a sheltering draw off the brooding Quitman Mountains, and left the draw an hour before the coming of the dawn to thread a pass and then to head between the Quitmans and Devil's Ridge looming toward the Eagle Mountains whose tallest peak showed hard against the dawning sky. It was empty country. The Rio Grande bordered it to the south, and beyond the Rio there was the vast, empty spaces of the northern part of the State of Chihuahua, Mexico.

The further southwest they rode the more relaxed became Buck's companion. They stayed the second night in a deserted *jacal* in the Sierra Viejas. Rorkin was now confident enough to let Buck build a fire against the cold of the mountain night. The fire had guttered low after the two men had taken to their blankets. A chilly wind crept in through the paneless windows and the empty doorway and stirred the thick layer of ashes in the beehive fireplace. Buck suddenly opened his eyes. He could hear Rorkin's gentle breathing. Buck turned his head. A faint red eye of ember stared back at him from the fireplace ashes. Buck closed his eyes, but there was a faint, insistent warning bell in the back of his mind. He opened his eyes again and thrust his socked feet out from under his blanket. He sat up and felt for his Winchester. Softly he padded to the nearest window, standing to one side of it to peer out into the cold, starlit night. It was quiet; it was almost too quiet. The wind was gone. Not a coyote howl broke the silence. The horses were in a small, tumble-down peeled-pole corral just behind the *jacal.*

"What is it, Spade?" softly asked Rorkin from his bed.

"I don't know."

"Nerves?" Rorkin laughed quietly. "The man of steel feeling nervous? You're safe enough from the law here."

"It isn't that," said Buck. "Quiet!"

"For God's sake get some sleep and let me get some too," said the outlaw.

The thin rear door was shattered by the hard, driving thrust of a boot heel. A dark figure charged right through the falling fragments toward Rorkin, lying helpless in his blankets. There was just enough light to show a thin sliver of polished steel extending from the man's hand. "Get the other one, Ramon!" the attacker yelled hoarsely in Spanish.

Buck whirled, levering home a round, to fire from the hip. The softnosed .44/40 slug caught the charging Mexican in the guts. He doubled over and the knife tinkled on the hardpacked earthen floor. Buck leaped through the open window, wincing as his socked feet landed in the shattered glass beneath it. A man was charging toward the open front doorway. Buck ran sideways, firing as he did so. The heavy slug caught the second man just about where the kidneys were located. He shrieked as the bullet drove him toward the wall of the *jacal*. He managed to turn and raise a pistol. It flashed and the slug picked insistently at the slack of Buck's shirt. A second shot whispered evilly just past his left ear. Buck fired his third shot. The man died on his feet and fell sideways across the open doorway.

Powder smoke rifted about Buck as he

walked toward the *jacal*. The echo of the last shots racketed away to die in the canyon behind the *jacal*. Rorkin was cursing fluently and viciously inside the *jacal*. Buck's dun whinnied sharply. Buck ran toward the corral. A third man was fighting to lead the two horses from the corral. The dun was rearing and plunging. Buck vaulted the low rail and landed ankle deep in thick warm manure. He fired twice as the horses plunged to one side leaving the man in the clear. The echoes of the two shots chased each other back and forth to get lost in the emptiness of the big canyon.

The man sank to his knees and held out pleading hands. "For the love of God, *señor*," he begged. "We wanted only the *caballos*." Blood dripped from his right hand into the filth of the corral. Buck looked down at him. The killing lust was still within him, but he lowered his smoking rifle. As he did so Rorkin came through the back doorway, pistol in hand and a look of hell on his face. As he did so a Mexican arose from a clump of brush beyond the *jacal* and raised a rifle to aim at him. Buck dropped bellyflat in the manure and fired upward. The rifleman shrieked as lead and rock shards slashed into his dark face. He jumped to

41

one side to meet the next shot which struck him in the chest and smashed him back onto his back. He did not move again.

Buck got slowly to his feet, cursing softly as he felt the fresh wet manure soaking through his thin shirt and worn levis. He looked at the Mexican who was still on his knees staring at Buck. "For love of God, *señores*," he pleaded. "Have pity! I am only a boy! I have never stolen anything before this time. By the Sweet Names, spare me, *señores!* You have killed my brother, my cousin and my best friend! Have pity!"

It was then that Powers Rorkin fired his only shot of the night. The slug caught the pleading boy full in his open mouth to shut it forever. Rorkin walked over to him and hooked a foot under his body to roll it over. The arms were outflung and the smashed and bloody face stared up at the outlaw with eyes that did not see. Rorkin gathered his spittle and spat full into the broken face.

Buck leaned on his rifle. The aftermath of violent killing was coming over him. The acrid odor of the manure hung about him, mingled with the stench of gunsmoke, while through it all, like a bright scarlet cord, was woven the odor of freshly spilled blood. Rorkin walked back into the *jacal*. Buck wiped most of the mess from his clothing and walked past the dead boy to the *jacal*. There was no sorrow in him for having killed three men in not many more minutes than three. More than a few times in his time as a trooper and later as a Ranger, he had seen what such roving *corridas* of *bandidos* had done to lone travelers or to isolated ranchers and their families. They were cold-blooded killers, without mercy, hated equally in Texas and in Chihuahua, and wanted by the law on both sides of the Rio Grande. The deaths of the three *bandidos* he had killed meant nothing. What bothered him now was the way Rorkin had murdered that helpless boy as the *muchacho* had pleaded for his life.

Rorkin looked up as Buck walked into the *jacal*. "I can't sleep after this, Cleburne," he said.

Buck threw some greasewood branches onto the ashes and blew hard on the ashes and embers. A tongue of flame licked up and danced happily along a branch. Buck looked back at Rorkin. "Conscience, Mister Rorkin?" he softly asked.

Rorkin's cold green eyes flicked at Buck.

"Hell no! They would have gutted us in our blankets if it hadn't been for you."

Buck began to refill his rifle magazine. "I've been on the owlhoot so long, it seems as though I've got a sixth sense, as they say, for such things. I didn't hear, see or smell 'em. I just *knew* they were there."

"A handy sense to have," said Rorkin. He eyed the Winchester. "You use that as good as you use a six-gun. You kill like a professional, Cleburne."

Buck looked down into the flickering flames. "Pass the bottle," he said over his shoulder. "Maybe I *am* a professional at that."

"Get rid of those clothes. You're about my build. I'll dig out some fresh clothing for you. I don't want a man to ride with my *corrida* unless he looks the part. Besides, you stink like a privy, Cleburne."

"*Gracias,*" said Buck dryly.

"*Por nada,*" said Rorkin politely. He began to dig into his saddlebags. He picked out fresh clothing and tossed it beside Spade. Buck pulled the cork out of the bottle with his teeth and drank deeply of the potent aguardiente. Brandy is the drink for heroes, he thought.

Rorkin laughed as he swung his gunbelt

about his waist, buckled it and settled it. He thrust his Colt into the holster. He laughed again as he took the bottle from the floor and drank deeply.

"What's the joke?" asked Buck as he finished dressing and pulled on his boots.

"I was thinking of the look on that kid's face when that slug of mine hit him in the *boca*," said Rorkin.

Buck laughed shortly. "Some joke," he said.

Rorkin looked closely at Buck for a second before he picked up his gear and his rifle and walked out of the *jacal*. They hauled the stiffening bodies into a gully beyond the *jacal* and dumped rocks in on top of them. Rorkin did a strange thing. He picked up the kid's dusty black sombrero and removed the heavy coin-silver hatband. He stuffed it into his pocket. It was hardly worth more than a few pesos at most, and little enough loot for a man like Powers Rorkin. There was just no accounting for tastes. The thought was in Buck Terrell's mind as he and Rorkin rode away southwesterly from that silent and isolated place of sudden death.

3

IT had turned unseasonably hot. A dry wind swept across the Big Bend country, moaning down the great canyons, and whining about the wolf-fanged peaks of the Santiagos and the Pena Blancas. In two days of steady riding the two men had not seen another human being. Veils of ochre dust swept across the faint trail they were following west of the Agua Frias. It had been a good many years since Buck Terrell had been in this country, although the first half of his army service had been in the area, riding out of Fort Davis to the north and Fort Leaton to the west, the latter being on the Rio Grande.

Now and again Buck would touch the ragged scar on his left cheek, souvenir of his service in the Big Bend country. Cibolo, where the Lipan buck had marked Buck for life, was hardly more than a day's ride behind them.

It was late afternoon, approaching dusk when Powers Rorkin thrust out an arm and pointed down a long ridge toward a willow bordered stream. A number of well-built adobes and *jacales* were on the far side of the stream, flanked by corrals. "Home, at least for the time being," he said.

Buck looked about in satisfaction. It was a good layout. Plenty of water. Grazing on the low land bordering the stream. Timber for firewood and building. Shelter from the winds.

"We ranch here," said Rorkin as he spurred his dun down the slope. He glanced sideways at Buck and a faint smile passed across his lean face. "A long way from the hand of the law. If they do poke around there are always the hills and the mountains, and the Rio Grande is only a hard day's ride to the south. We don't plan our work that way though." He tapped the side of his head. "Plan your work and work your plan. That's our motto."

The dying sun glinted on something high on the ridge to the right. Buck glanced at it. Rorkin lighted a cigar. "I might add that we have been under field-glass surveillance for the past twenty minutes. If they hadn't recognized me, we would have been stopped back at the entrance to the valley."

"Very neat," said Buck.

Rorkin looked at him. "Another thing: The

47

boys are choosey and have a way of making a man prove himself. I'll talk you up, naturally, and with good reason, but the boys live on the wrong side of the law, and we take no chances on weak sisters or traitors. You follow me?"

"I get the idea."

They crossed the creek on a plank bridge and turned toward the buildings. A thread of smoke wavered up from the cookhouse. A horse whinnied in the corral. A door slammed inside one of the buildings. A dog barked harshly and was joined by several others, and then four dogs trotted toward the two horsemen. Buck's eyes narrowed. He had seen rough dogs in his day, but this quartet seemed to be handpicked for power and viciousness.

They looked at Rorkin and then at Buck, and it seemed to him they were looking right through flesh and bone into the very soul of him.

"Our special guards," said Rorkin. "Pancho, Hammerhead, Sam and Lizzie. Let me tell you, Liz is the worst of the bunch. The female of the species, you know."

Buck nodded. "I think I know what you mean," he said.

Rorkin relighted his cigar. "They'll get to

48

know you after awhile, but until they do, don't take any chances with them."

"I wasn't intending to."

They dismounted beside the biggest of the adobes, and the four brutes sniffed suspiciously about Buck's heels, sending a cold shiver up his spine. They would know him now, and it seemed to him that they might know his secret before the men did.

A tall man leaned against the side of the doorway as Rorkin and Buck approached the house. "You're back early, Boss," he said.

"Had to hurry up a bit, Moss."

The dark eyes narrowed. "Trouble with the law?"

"Not on my account. This is Spade Cleburne. He might be joining us. Moss Beckett, Spade, my right hand man."

The hard eyes flicked up and down Spade. "Howdy," said Moss. "Where do you hail from, Cleburne?"

"Texas."

"What part of Texas?"

Buck smiled faintly. "Just *Texas*, mister."

"Yeh." Moss opened the door behind him and stepped to one side to let them enter and his eyes studied Buck as Buck passed inside after Rorkin.

There were three more men in the big room. Two of them sat at a table playing cards, while the third sprawled in a chair near the fireplace, staring at the cold ashes.

"*Amigos*, this is Spade Cleburne," said Rorkin. "Might be one of us."

Three pairs of eyes studied Buck. One of the card players wore an ornate Mex steeple crowned hat, heavy with coin silver, but he wasn't a Mexican. He stood up and thrust out a hand toward Buck. "Tod Logan," he said shortly. His hand gripped Buck's like a vise, feeling for a weakness. His black eyes seemed to indicate some Indian blood.

The second card player was shuffling the deck. "Cap Anthony," he said casually. "You a card player, Cleburne?"

"Sometimes," said Buck.

Anthony was lean and long, without an ounce of fat on him, from his thin face to his long feet. A feeling of coldness, of almost complete impersonality seemed to emanate from him. He gave Buck a chill almost similar to that which the dogs had given him. The man's eyes were a curious light gray, and they seemed nonhuman to Buck, as though the man was some alien being in human guise. Cap was busy with the cards again, his slim brown fingers working them with incredible mechanical speed and dexterity.

"My younger brother Gil," said Rorkin.

Buck turned. The man in the chair had stood up, and the resemblance to Powers Rorkin was stamped on his face, although he was at least ten to twelve years younger than his brother. Where the older brother's face was hard and set, stronger and disciplined, there was a look about Gil that indicated that he had been badly spoiled, used to his own way, and a sonofabitch if he did not get it. His clothes were of finer quality than the others wore, well cut and expensive, and it was a cinch he never rode the range in them. Not in West Texas at least.

Gil Rorkin nodded. His eyes flicked down toward the low-slung, plain walnut-handled Colt, and then up at Buck's face as though to gauge him for some secret reason of his own.

"Gil is the fastest gun in the Big Bend country," said Powers Rorkin.

"In *Texas*," corrected Gil quickly.

Tod Logan coughed and Gil's eyes seemed to bore a hole through the smoky air. Cap

51

Anthony was dealing and his eyes never left the cards.

"Cleburne is pretty good too," said Powers casually. He relighted his cigar. "That's why I brought him along."

"So?" said Gil quietly. His eyes were fixed on Buck, as though a new cock had walked into the hen yard to challenge the reigning rooster.

Moss Beckett was standing just behind Buck now. There was a tension in the smoky air, just as there had been outside when the dogs had sniffed about Buck as he had dismounted.

"Let us in on it, Boss," said Tod Logan. "Two cards, Cap."

Powers Rorkin swiftly told them of the killing in Chico's *cantina* in Aguila and of the death of the four bravos back in the lonely Sierra Vieja.

"You're getting careless, Powers," said Gil. "Letting them Mexes sneak up on you like that. Now, if *I* had been along . . ."

"You couldn't have done any better than Spade did," said Tod Logan.

Gil's cold eyes flicked from Buck to Tod. "What do you mean?" he said.

Tod shrugged. "Four Mexes. Bing! Bing! Bing! Bing! Just like that, and they were four *good* Mexes. How can *you* top that kind'a gunplay, Gil?"

Gil flushed. "I would'a done the same then! Besides, I don't count Mexes!"

Tod shrugged again. "But *you* wasn't there, Gil." His flat, hard face was impassive, but Buck had a feeling he was needling Gil.

"Shut up the two of you," said Powers.

"One of these days . . ." said Gil. He looked again at Buck, his shallow brain having dismissed Tod as of no consequence, at the moment anyway. "Let's see that fast draw, Cleburne."

Buck looked at Powers. Powers' face was enigmatic.

"Go on, Cleburne," urged Gil. "Draw!"

Buck stepped back and then clawed down for a draw and as his hand came up with the Colt he found himself facing two nickel-plated and engraved Colts that had sprung into the kid's slim hands as though growing out of them and even as Buck watched incredulously the twin Colts roared, spitting flame and smoke. The soft-nosed forty/fours rapped into the thick wall behind Buck and to either side of him and he could have sworn he felt the invisible passage of those twin messengers of death past his sleeves.

Gil peered through the rising smoke quietly smiling, waiting for Buck to speak. A cold trickle of sweat worked its way down the middle of Buck's back. "You're fast, Gil," he admitted hoarsely, and he wasn't buttering the kid up either.

Gil grinned. "You guys see? He's fast! Powers said so! Didn't I beat him to the draw by seconds?"

"Yup," said Tod, "but he wasn't trying to *kill* you, Gil. Makes a difference when a man is up against a fast gun who's willing to *kill*."

In the silence that followed there was death in Gil's eyes as he looked at the imperturbable Tod Logan, who was dealing swiftly.

"Put away those Colts, Kid," said Powers quietly.

It was then that Buck noticed the latent madness in the Kid's eyes, the almost insane homicidal look, and another chill swept over his body. A copperhead might have more feeling for life than would the Kid.

"Gil!" snapped Powers.

Gil slowly slid the fancy six-guns back into their ornately carved sheaths. The hovering madness was still in his eyes. Then he walked slowly toward Buck. "You saw me shoot," he said thickly. "You ever see another gun as fast as me?"

Buck wanted to walk away from the young man, for he could almost smell death.

"You hear me?" said Gil. His unblinking eyes stared at Buck.

Buck could not resist. "Only one," he said.

"Who?" snarled Gil.

Buck timed it perfectly. "Name of John Wesley Hardin," he said casually. "You ever hear of him?"

Tod Logan guffawed. Cap Anthony's expression never changed. Powers Rorkin flushed a little. A secretive, and appreciative smile fled across Moss Beckett's brown face.

"A comedian, eh?" said Gil in a low voice. "A real funny fellow. Haw! Haw! Haw! I ought'a ram a hot gun muzzle down your throat, Cleburne."

"Don't try it," said Buck coldly.

Again came the long, pregnant silence.

"What did you say?" said Gil at last.

Powers Rorkin walked between them. "Get outside, Kid, and cool off," he said. "Cleburne saved my life. I won't have the two of you arguing. Not in my *corrida* anyway."

Gil stalked to the door and left the room. The

door slammed behind him. Tod Logan looked up at Powers. "He's getting more loco every day," he said. "One of these days he's going to get us all killed. You remember that Ranger . . ." His voice trailed off as he saw the silencing look on Powers' face.

"He's all right," said Powers. "High spirits is all."

Buck looked at the bullet pocks in the wall. "Yeah," he said softly, "high spirits."

"Tod may be right," said Moss Beckett. "The Kid loses his head any time anyone questions his fast draw."

Rorkin walked to the fireplace and rolled a cigarette. "He's my brother," he said over his shoulder.

Beckett waved a hand. "Sure, Boss, but you know how he gets. He's got what they call an obs . . . an obser . . . oh *hell!*"

"Obsession," said Buck. He took out the makings and began to fashion a smoke. He still had the feeling that they had been testing him. "*The boys are choosey and have a way of making a man prove himself. We take no chances on weak sisters or traitors,*" Rorkin had said.

"He'll work out all right," said Rorkin. "I've got a place for him in the master plan."

Buck lit his cigarette and glanced curiously at Rorkin. The man had tried to make it sound convincing. Certainly Gil Rorkin was a fast gun, as fast, or faster than any man Buck had seen, with the exception of John Wesley Hardin, and it was certainly no disgrace to any man to be compared to him. Rorkin sounded as though he was defending Gil when he, himself knew all the time that Gil was dangerous not only to their enemies, but to themselves. Already Buck had spotted a weak link in the chain. There was hostility between some of the members of the *corrida* as well. Tough boots such as these men would hardly knuckle down to any man. They accepted each other as equals perhaps, but never as superiors. Yet Powers Rorkin had some hold on them. Perhaps it was his mind, his superior intelligence that gave him his leading position. They were fighting men and killers, beyond the pale of the law, but they evidently knew they had to have a plan and a man to plan for them. That man was Powers Rorkin, and it seemed as though his only weakness was one of blood ties, that of his brother Gil.

Moss Beckett walked to the door. "I'll show you your quarters, Cleburne," he said.

Buck followed him outside. It was dusk. The wind had shifted. The windmill was whirring steadily. The tantalizing odor of cooking food drifted on the wind.

"How often does the Kid get riled up like that?" asked Buck.

Beckett did not answer. He walked under the *ramada* that ran the length of the northern half of the big *casa*. He opened a door and walked into the room.

Buck walked in behind the man. "I asked you a question," he said.

"I heard you," said Beckett. He lit a lamp. The flaring yellow light revealed a small room furnished with washstand, narrow bed, wall cupboard and a dusty rug on the earthen floor.

"Well?" said Buck.

Beckett turned. "Gil is one of us," he said quietly. "Who are *you*, mister?"

"Spade Cleburne," said Buck.

"Yeh, Spade . . . Spade Cleburne. A nice fitting handle for a stranger comin' in here. Well, *Mister* Cleburne, let me tell you that you ain't one of *us*, not yet. Gil Rorkin *is* one of us. He's got his faults. We all have. But we

58

trust him as much as we trust each other."
Beckett smiled faintly. "We *have* to trust each
other in this business, Cleburne. I don't know
you yet, but I'd go to hell in a bread basket for
Powers Rorkin, and don't you ever forget it."

Beckett walked to the door. "The crapper is
around the back," he said over his shoulder.
"Bath house is beyond the cooking *jacal*. We
eat in about an hour." He closed the door
behind him and Buck heard the popping of his
bootheels die away toward the southern end of
the long adobe.

Buck flipped his cigarette butt into the little
fireplace and rolled himself another one which
he lighted. He scaled his hat at a wall hook and
watched it settle on the hook, to swing idly to
and fro. He dropped flat on the bed and locked
his hands behind his neck. There was something Tod Logan had said that had stuck in
Buck's mind. *"He's getting more loco every
day. One of these days he's going to get us all
killed. You remember that Ranger . . ."*

"Which Ranger?" said Buck aloud.

There was something else he remembered.
The words of Dan Lynch at his secret meeting
with Buck in Chico's *cantina*. "I mean that
Rangers have been murdered out here in line of

59

duty. Not killed, Buck, but murdered in cold blood! How do you feel about that, Mister Terrell?"

He closed his eyes and conjured up the picture Dan Lynch had painted verbally for him. Frank, Buck's younger brother, had been murdered by a person or persons unknown. Ranger Armenderiz had been hardly recognizable when they had found his mutilated body near Maravillas Creek. Ranger Durkee had been hung to a tree near Tornillo Draw, recognizable only by a bullet scar on his left thigh. Ranger Ledbetter, one of Buck's oldest and best friends, had been tortured by being driven through tornillo and catclaw, then dragged to his death over razor-edged rocks and through the stabbing needles of the thorny growths in that rough country. They had left his battered corpse in the road near Terlingua Creek with a tin star stuck to his naked chest with a Mexican *cuchillo*.

Buck drew in on the cigarette and the glowing of the tip lighted the hard, lean face, with the ragged scar, but it was the eyes that would have given a chill of impending death to anyone who was watching Buck Terrell.

There was something else that had stuck in

his mind like a burr to a saddle blanket. How Powers Rorkin had killed the Mex kid who was lying helpless in the filth of the corral, and what he had done after that; the taking of the cheap coin-silver band from the sweat-stained hat of the dead boy, after they had hastily buried him with his three partners in thievery. There was a sadistic touch in Powers Rorkin, and it was present also in the twisted mind of his brother Gil.

Buck flipped the cigarette into the fireplace and arose to wash himself. He looked at his face in the cracked mirror. There wasn't any doubt but what he had changed considerably since his days in West Texas. The scar had somehow transformed his face into a different semblance, but there was something he had added to it himself. He had seen death eye-to-eye too many times in the past years. A man working behind the star can become as callous to death as any cold-blooded killer, but somehow it leaves invisible scars on his soul. He steeled his nerve as he combed his thick, reddish hair, and dusted off his trail clothing. There was a job to be done. So far so good. He had entered the den of the lobos. One false step, one forgetful instant and he'd die as the other four Rangers had died. Five graves, instead of four, to waiting Boot Hill, silvery lighted by the moon, and as cold as death itself.

He stepped outside and saw a broad-shouldered man, wearing a Mex hat, swinging down from a blocky gray. For an instant he thought it might be Tod Logan, but this man was thicker through the chest. He moved like a hunting cat as he walked toward Buck. "Is the Boss around?" he asked, and there was no mistaking his origin. His accent betrayed his birth, but there was no softness in his speech. His voice rang metallically. He stopped and peered at Buck, and his hand drifted down to a sheathed *cuchillo* at his side. "Who are you?" he asked.

"Spade Cleburne. I came in with Mister Rorkin this afternoon."

"I do not know of you, *hombre*."

Buck shrugged. "Nor I of you, *hombre*."

The dark eyes studied Buck from beneath the wide brim of the dusty hat. "We have met somewhere before perhaps?"

"Not to my knowledge."

"So. I am Blas Perez. The boys call me *Cuchillo*."

"*Knife?* It is an odd name."

"Not for Blas Perez, *hombre*."

"That you, Cuchillo?" called Moss Beckett from the end of the *ramada*.

"Yes, *amigo*."

"The Boss is here. He's been waiting for you."

"And I for him, *amigo*."

Blas touched the brim of his hat to Buck. "See you later," he said. "Your name please?"

"Spade Cleburne."

Blas smiled just a little. "You thought my nickname was odd. Spade? Is that not an odd name also?"

"It is my real name, Blas."

Blas nodded. He walked toward Moss Beckett.

Buck fashioned a cigarette. The picture of Kelly Ledbetter lying dead in the road with a tin star, roughly shaped like a Ranger star, held to his chest by the thin blade of a Mex *cuchillo*, came back to him.

The wind shifted and the windmill slowed down and then stopped as the wind played about a bit and then died away. From the distant hills came the faint, melancholy crying of a coyote, and he was no lonelier, and a good deal less nervous than

Buck Terrell, alias Spade Cleburne, sitting in the middle of a nest of cold-blooded human diamondbacks.

4

THE high-riding moon was on the wane. Far below the castellated ridge that bordered the rough road, the canyon was already in darkness. The pass to the north, just above the crossing of the Rio Grande, was still lighted clearly. A stretch of the river could be seen from the heights of the ridge, flowing like a pewter trace until it vanished between towering walls of rock that encroached on the river from both the Texas and Coahuila sides of the Rio Grande.

It was very quiet on the heights except for the faint and dry scrabbling of the night wind. Buck Terrell shifted a little and peered down into the canyon. His ears had picked up a different sound from that of the wind. He looked back over his shoulder. Higher up the ridge was Tod Logan and Cap Anthony, while below Buck, and to the right, was Moss Beckett. Somewhere in the thick darkness to the left was Gil Rorkin.

Buck wet his dry lips. He peered down

through the darkness and saw a steeple-crowned hat bob up and down, then a man whistled softly three times, then three times again, followed by a pause, then two sharp high-pitched notes floated on the night air. It was Blas Perez.

Buck shoved back his hat. It wasn't the ten-gallon hat Powers Rorkin had given him back at the ranch. It was a heavy, sweat soaked Mexican hat. All the others who did not ordinarily wear such hats wore them this night on the Mexican side of the Rio Grande. Buck had on a Mex jacket as well. His face was dark enough in the shadow of the brim to pass for a Mexican. That was the general idea, as outlined by Powers Rorkin, when he had divulged his plan for quick money and no strings attached. He had made a deal with Bernardo Sanchez, local bandit chieftain from further west, in the State of Chihuahua, while in El Paso. It seemed as though smugglers were using this river crossing for their undercover and strictly illegal business on the Texas side of the river. Both the Texas Rangers and the Guardia Rurale were on the watch for these men. Powers Rorkin had made his plans well. False information had been relayed to the Rangers and the Rurales, taking them miles from the crossing this particular night. There would be no trouble from the Rangers on the American side of the Rio, nor none from the Rurales on the Mexican side of it.

Blas scrambled over the rocks and dropped down beside Moss Beckett. "They have crossed the Rio," he said breathlessly. "Sanchez is in position on the other side of the pass. He knows Parado, the leader of the smugglers. Sanchez will delay him on the road just below us."

"How many men does Parado have?" asked Beckett.

"Fifteen."

"And Sanchez?"

"Only four. Some of his men did not reach here yet."

Moss whistled softly. "Parado is no push-over," he said. "We don't want too much shooting. We don't know for sure if there are any Rurales in the area."

"Sanchez says no."

"I don't trust Sanchez!" snapped Moss.

Blas shrugged. "We have no choice," he said.

"I don't like it," said Moss.

"*Señor* Rorkin has made a good plan," said Blas.

"Yeh, but he's not here to take any of the punishment if anything goes wrong."

"His brother is," said Cuchillo.

Moss rubbed his lean jaw. He eyed the darkened canyon. It would be a touchy business. If the Rurales caught them down there they'd never make it to the river. "I wish to God we could have worked this out by ourselves," snarled Moss. "Sanchez isn't reliable in my book."

"We need his help," said Blas simply. "What else can we do?"

"Let's get on with it," said another voice.

Buck turned. Gil Rorkin was standing behind the two men, leaning on his rifle. "Get down," Buck said sharply.

Gil ignored him. "Powers said we can trust Sanchez," he said. "At least until we get the loot." He grinned.

"You're lined against the sky," warned Buck.

Gil glanced casually at him. "Shut up," he said. "I take no orders from you or anyone else around here."

Moss Beckett's face tightened. "I had an idea I was in charge around here," he said.

"Well, you ain't doing your job," said Gil sarcastically.

Something echoed from the north end of the canyon. Buck looked toward the pass. Clearly seen in the light of the moon was a string of burros, trotting rapidly down toward the darker part of the canyon, escorted by more than a dozen big-hatted men riding beside them, carbines butted against their hips. It was the party of Parado the smuggler. There was no time to argue further. The die was cast.

"Let's go, *amigos*," said Gil. He plunged down the slope toward the unseen road far below.

"God damn him!" snapped Beckett. "He's jumped the gun!"

Tod Logan stood up and looked down toward the disappearing form of Gil Rorkin. "One of these days that damned fool will get us all killed. You mark my words."

Cap Anthony looked at Moss. "Well," he said casually, "do we go after him?"

"There is no other choice," said Cuchillo.

"Let's go then," said Beckett. "*Adelante!*" There was a taut bitterness on his lean face.

In fifteen minutes they were in position at the south end of the canyon, while across the dark road were the men of Sanchez. Hoof beats sounded on the hard rutted road. A horse whinnied. Then through the gathering darkness appeared the party of smugglers, urging on their laden burros in unholy haste to get away from the river and into the hidden canyons of the Serranias del Burro.

The smugglers were within fifty yards of the ambushers when a sharp whistle sounded above the thudding of the hoofs. The canyon became alive with spitting flames and the echoes awoke shudderingly as gun shot after gun shot slammed against the walls of the great trough in the harsh earth. Smoke arose and hung above the road while screaming men died beneath the thrashing, kicking burros and maddened horses. They had no chance at all. It was unadulterated murder.

Buck Terrell emptied his rifle high above the heads of the dying men and horses. It was too dark for anyone to see where he was shooting, and his guts churned within him as he heard the death cries of the Mexicans. There was no one to hear them except the men who were wiping them out like ants.

It was all over in five minutes. The smoke drifted off down the valley after the dying echoes of the shooting. There were other sounds. The crying out of the wounded men and the more terrible sounds made by the horses who were also wounded.

Spurs jingled as the Americans and the Mexicans walked down into that bloody road of death. It was then that Buck saw Gil Rorkin, his face lighted by an unholy drive as he stalked toward the nearest of the downed smugglers.

"Wait!" said Moss Beckett.

Gil turned and his Colts were in his slim hands. "Why?" he snarled.

Moss looked down at the twin muzzles and then up into those mad eyes. He was a brave man but even the bravest of men quail before a mad dog.

"Let him go ahead," said Sanchez as he reloaded his smoking rifle. He grinned at Moss. "*Los muertos no hablan*," he added. "I myself have had enough of killing for this night. There is not much time, *amigo*."

"Let him have his blood letting," said Tod Logan quietly. "It's his food and drink."

Even as Tod's words still sounded on the air the twin Colts cracked. Two holes appeared as if by magic in the sweat dewed face of one of the smugglers. Ten more shots cracked out, tumbling head over heels after each other and each leaden chunk killed a wounded man or

71

horse. It made no difference to Gil Rorkin. Blood was blood, animal or human. When he reached the end of the blood-dyed trail there wasn't a living thing lying on the road, nothing but the bodies of fifteen men and fifteen horses, sown with hot lead as a farmer sows a field. *Los muertos no hablan*. The dead do not talk.

Buck tasted sour bile in the back of his throat. He looked away from the evil grinning face of Gil Rorkin as the Kid reloaded his handsome Colts, his messengers of cold-blooded death.

"Go get the horses, Spade," said Moss. "Give him a hand, Tod."

Buck walked up the darkened slopes with Tod just behind him. "You ever see the like?" said Tod. He shook his head.

Buck could take no chances with any of these killers. "They had to be shut up," he said. "One way or another."

"Sure! Sure! But Gil has to *wade* in blood! Jesus God! Some of us get our kicks out of booze, others out of wimmen, but that bastard craves blood like a drunk craves booze."

They reached the top of the ridge and walked down the far side toward the picketed horses. "What now?" said Buck.

Tod shrugged. "We pull leather for the Rio," he said.

"Leaving them there?"

"Who's to know who did it? Sanchez is from up Chihuahua way. He'll ride across the Rio with us tonight, then vanish. Any one sees us in these Mex getups will think we're local *bandidos* cutting up a few touches. Besides, what do the Rurales care? Fifteen less smugglers to deal with. Saves time, horseflesh and money."

"Yeah," said Buck. "I never thought of it quite that way."

"Powers Rorkin has a brain," said the burly outlaw. "Before I joined up with him I made about three hundred dollars profit in seven robberies. Lived from hand to mouth, chased and chivvied all over West Texas until Rorkin offered me a chance to ride with him."

"And since then?" said Buck. He started leading some of the horses down the slope.

"I've done all right."

"More than three hundred dollars?"

"Sure!"

"In your pockets?"

Logan looked curiously at Buck. "Why, hellsfire, Cleburne, we haven't even got *started*

73

yet! Give Rorkin time to get his master plan into operation."

"I don't know anything about that."

"Neither do the rest of us, but when he lets us know we'll be the big wheels in this part of the country I tell you! That's *one* bet you can damned well copper!"

Buck did not speak again. *The master plan.* In the ten days he had been with the Rorkin *corrida* he had heard that phrase mentioned time and time again, but none of them, with the exception of Rorkin himself, seemed to know anything about it, and that included Gil Rorkin. These hard-gutted fighting men trusted in the brains and planning skills of Powers Rorkin, and that was that. *The master plan.*

"Gawdalmighty," said Cap Anthony as Tod Logan and Buck brought up the horses. "They's over twenty thousand in gold in Parado's bags!"

Tod Logan stared at him. "You're joshing!"

"So help me God, *amigo!*"

"Anything else?"

"Over a hundred Colt six-shooters in factory grease and fifty Winchesters the same way, loaded on the burros."

74

"What the hell good are they?" Tod spat to one side. "We got all the guns we need."

Anthony looked toward the place where Moss Beckett and Bernardo Sanchez were in deep consultation. "Sanchez wants the pistols and rifles for part of his share of the loot. Moss told him he could have them, but he'd have to be satisfied with less than half of the gold." Anthony grinned. "Ol' Bernardo he don't like that at all."

Sanchez' men were standing near the laden burros watching their leader arguing with Moss Beckett and their dark faces were clouded with hate. Ten thousand in gold was a fortune in Mexico and they meant to have their share of it.

Moss at last slapped his hand against his thigh. "I can't do it, Sanchez," he said firmly. "It's up to Rorkin to make the decision. You've got to cross the Rio tonight anyway before the Rurales come chargin' up here. You come along with us to the rancho and see Rorkin."

Bernardo Sanchez threw up his hands in disgust. "All right then!" he said. "Let's go! *Adelante!*"

They all mounted and rode north up the

75

canyon and none of them looked back at the stiffening blue-faced men in the bloody road.

The moon still shone faintly on the river. The river was low and this was a fair fording place. Moss Beckett let Gil Rorkin, Cuchillo and Cap Anthony go ahead, while Sanchez and his quartet of men drove the burros across, belly deep in the silvered water, while Moss, Tod Logan and Buck waited on the Mexican bank as a rear guard. There was no sight nor sound of any others in that lonely country. It was likely that the shooting had not been heard. It was also quite likely that some days would pass before the wheeling *zopilotes* would guide the curious to the canyon of death.

Moss Beckett started across the river when Sanchez and his men began urging the tired, heavily laden burros up the muddy American bank, lashing and cursing at the beasts. Gil, Cuchillo and Cap sat their mounts just beyond the mud of the bank, smoking and idly watching the Mexicans as they worked. Gil raised his head and looked toward the three Americans fording the river. The burros were all out of the water now. Moss Beckett suddenly raised his hat and swung it in a circle. The action triggered the explosion of three rifles.

Bernardo Sanchez fell heavily in the mud, squirming and thrashing.

Two of his men fell and lay still. The third spurred his mount back toward the Mexican side. Cap Anthony waited until he was fifty feet from the shore then fired once. The Mexican slid from his wet horse without a sound and vanished below the silvered surface of the river. The last of the Mexicans ran along the muddy bank, then plunged into the Rio, swimming strongly for the Mexican side while caught in the fluid strength of the current. The gun shot echoes died away. A burro brayed thinly.

"Fifty bucks I can hit him the first shot," said Tod Logan easily.

"You're on," said Gil Rorkin.

Logan raised his rifle and fired. The bullet jetted the water a foot to one side of the struggling Mexican. It was excellent shooting, but Gil Rorkin laughed. He raised his rifle with hardly taking time to aim and fired once. The echo of the shot fled down the river and the Mexican sank like a stone. "Pay me, Logan," sneered Gil.

Sanchez was mouthing weak curses as he tried to get to his feet. Gil eyed him. "You want a sporting chance, Bernardo?" he coldly asked.

"Damn you to hell!" mouthed the wounded man.

"Start out, *hombre*," said Gil thinly. He pointed his rifle toward the far shore.

Sanchez got weakly to his feet. "Go to hell, *gringo*," he snarled. His defiance was punctuated by the sound of Gil's rifle and the slug hit Sanchez in the head. He fell backward into the shallows. The current tugged gently at his body, worked him loose, floated him for fifty feet then enveloped him forever.

Moss Beckett urged his gray out of the river. "Let's cache the rifles and pistols," he said.

It took an hour to get the cased weapons into hiding and well concealed by loose rock and brush. Two of the burros, laden with the gold, were led up into the canyon. The remainder died by gunfire after they were driven belly deep into the river. Then Moss Beckett led his bloody-handed crew into the fastnesses of the tangled mountains that bordered the Rio Grande.

Buck Terrell rode silently, a cigarette pasted in the corner of his thin mouth. He had never before seen such cold blooded and efficient slaughter. Twenty men had died that night under the guns of merciless men. Twenty thousand in gold was being carried back to the greedy hands of Powers Rorkin. A thousand dollars a man. Jesus Christ himself had not rated such betrayal money. There was no way to bring these killers to justice. What cared the Rurales about the deaths of such men as Parado and his crew of smugglers? They were as bloody as any other outlaws who rode the Rio Grande banks. Nor would Bernardo Sanchez and his men ever speak against the Rorkin *corrida*. Who cared about them? Rorkin's plan had worked to perfection, for he had not lost a man, and had gained twenty thousand dollars for the price of betrayal.

Yet twenty thousand dollars was hardly enough for a crew like Rorkin's if it was equally divided amongst them. That was what was puzzling Buck Terrell as he rode north that night through the tangled mazes of the Sierra del Caballo Muerto, with the little burros trotting steadily along amidst the outlaws. Tod Logan had just as much as said he had received little or no pay from riding with Rorkin. "Give Rorkin time to get his master plan into operation," he had said.

Thirty miles from the rancho, Moss Beckett

called a halt. "We split up here," he said. "Cuchillo and me will drive the burros back to the rancho. Tod and Cap will head for the Chisos. Gil, you take Spade. Head north until late this afternoon, then west. Come back to the rancho within the next two days."

Gil rolled a cigarette and nodded.

"Stay out of trouble," added Beckett. "Be seen, but keep your mouths shut."

"Who was aiming to get into trouble?" said Cap Anthony.

"Yeh," said Tod Logan. He swiveled his eyes toward Gil.

Buck tightened his cinch. He glanced sideways at Gil.

Gil lighted his cigarette and his curious eyes flicked about the circle of hard faces. "Moss means me," he said. "Is that why you saddled me with Cleburne, Moss? To keep my nose clean?"

"It was your brother's orders," said the tall man.

Gil nodded. "Just you head back to the rancho with them burros," he said quietly.

Moss flushed beneath his tan. "What the hell you mean by that?" he demanded.

Gil shrugged. He swung up into his saddle. "You heard me, Beckett," he said thinly. "By God, I got a good mind to dip my fingers into that gold to stake me for a high lonesome in town."

Beckett eyed the kid. "I got my orders," he said flatly.

Gil leaned an elbow on his saddle horn and eyed the tall man. "I killed most of them, didn't I?" he said.

Tod Logan snorted. "While they couldn't shoot back," he said.

Gil's face whitened and his mouth worked a little. For an instant it looked as though he was going to draw on Logan.

Buck swung up into his saddle and rode slowly in between Gil and Tod. "Come on," he said. "I don't aim to sit around here all night. I want some chile and beans and maybe a bottle or two of beer, and I sure as hell don't know how to find 'em myself. Come on, Gil. Show me the way."

They rode up a narrow draw and as they rode the rest of the men watched them. Tod Logan looked down at his rifle. "One shot would do it," he said softly. "Who'd talk?"

No one answered. They looked at each other

out of the corners of their eyes. The same idea had flitted through their minds at almost the same time.

5

BUCK TERRELL sat at a table in the low ceilinged *cantina*, nursing his third bottle of beer, trying to shut out the sickening voice of Gil Rorkin from his ears and his thoughts. All that day, the day after the raid on the smugglers, he had been forced to listen to Gil mouthing off, talking a big wind. He held his temper in check at the insinuating remarks of the braggart, listening over and over again to how *he*, Gil Rorkin, the best and fastest gun in Texas, had personally done all the killing, or at least most of the killing during the bloody events of the night before. Buck had listened, hoping the kid would reveal some clue or another about the deaths, or rather murders of the four Rangers who had preceded Buck into this country of violence. Somehow or another, a checkrein of instinctive guile seemed to hold Gil back from making any incriminating statements about anything that had happened in the past, because of the still present glare of the shooting and killing along the Rio Grande. It had been then that Buck had realized that Gil Rorkin's quest for blood and glory made the most recent events important and shadowed out the past, except for the fact that they were a lower course of bricks in the building of the tremendous and warped ego of the man.

Buck looked toward the end of the long bar where Gil was leaning casually against the mahogany, a glass in his hand, twin Colts slung low and tied down, hat slanted across his somewhat handsome face, talking up a storm about the best guns in Texas, with the unspoken insinuation that *he*, of course, belonged to the matchless company of the same. In half an hour he had spoken of them all. Bill Longley, a legend even in his time, supposed to have survived his ultimate hanging by means of a trick harness concealed beneath his shirt, later to be "resurrected" and to vanish into the mists of legend. John Wesley Hardin the greatest of the "Texas Guns" who had supposedly killed forty men, and who was now serving time in Huntsville. Ben Thompson the "Wizard of the Pistol," Confederate soldier, gambler, law officer and outlaw, English by birth but Texan by choice and fearless to the end. There were others. King Fisher, Jim Miller, Dallas Stoudenmire, long-haired Jim Courtright, Bass Outlaw, and many others, all of them named as a brilliant backdrop for the heir apparent to the mantle of *The* Texas Gun, one Gil Rorkin.

Buck eyed the other men in the place. It was surprisingly well patronized for the remote area in which it was situated. There were six men at the bar, four at a table, and two drunks sleeping it off in back booths, while the principal talker, indeed the only talker, was Gil Rorkin. He didn't drink much; he didn't have to, thought Buck.

Buck wondered idly how many men Gil had actually killed and he wondered with more than idleness if he had killed any of the four Rangers whom Buck had sworn to avenge. Perhaps he had even killed Frank Terrell. There wasn't any doubt in Buck's mind that Gil Rorkin was faster on the draw than Buck was, and as accurate a shot as he had ever seen, but something Tod Logan had said came back to Buck as he sat there listening to Gil's droning talk. "Makes a difference when a man is up against a fast gun who's willing to *kill*." Buck had not yet seen Gil face a man to match draws, with the penalty of slowness being death.

"Always struck me peculiar why the Rangers

don't do anything about losing four of their men in this country. It ain't like the Rangers to do that," a gray-haired man said as he refilled his whisky glass.

Buck's head snapped up.

Another man lit a cigar and blew out a cloud of smoke. "Hell," he said around the thick butt of the cigar, "they don't like the Big Bend and they aim to let it alone. Which is all right with me."

A short man shook his head. "You mark my words," he said. "They haven't forgotten the deaths of those four men. Murders they were, pure and simple. Bad enough a Ranger gets shot down in a gun fight, but to murder a Ranger is like moving into Death Row at Huntsville. They'll get you, sooner or later, one way or another."

Gil Rorkin laughed. "There aren't enough Rangers to cover this country. They haven't got the guts to send any more of their men in. Big brag, the Rangers. Charge hell with a bucket of water and all that. One Ranger against a hundred outlaws? Hell, don't worry, pick the *nearest* outlaw and charge!" He slapped a hand on the bar so that the glass and bottles leaped. He laughed shrilly.

86

"All the same," said the short man, "you can bet your bottom dollar they'll be comin' around again, and they won't stop comin' around until they clean out the men who done those four Rangers in."

Gil eyed the little man. "Justin," he said coldly. "I said there weren't enough Rangers to cover this country. You say they'll be coming around. You making a liar out of me?"

Justin paled a little. "Why, no, Gil, I happen to know the record of the Rangers. You know as well as I do they won't let anyone get away with wiping out four of their men. Wiping out one is bad enough, but four is adding insult to injury. That's all I was saying."

"You see any of them around?" demanded Gil.

"No," admitted Justin.

Gil emptied his glass. "Maybe you think one of them will walk in here, star and all, to ask questions about them four killings?"

"How would I know?"

"You seem to know a lot," said Gil thinly.

It grew very quiet in the saloon. Gil was now badgering Justin, not just disagreeing with him. The signs were plain enough. Justin, even if he was right and sure of himself, should have known better than to disagree with a man like Gil Rorkin.

"Justin didn't mean anything," said the bartender.

"Keep your nose out of this, Charley," said Gil.

Justin smiled weakly. He held out a small hand. "I'm sorry, Gil," he said. He swallowed a little.

Gil slapped the hand out of the way. Justin looked from side to side. The situation had taken a turn he had not expected. "I'll be going now," he said.

Gil raised his right foot and planted the cruel heel on Justin's instep. "Wait," he said quietly. "I want you to empty this bottle with me, so's I know you ain't unhappy with me."

One of the men laughed. The bartender shook his head.

Justin wet his dry lips. "You know I ain't supposed to drink too much, Gil. A beer or two is all I'm allowed."

"You can have a snort or two of red eye."

"You know what it does to me, Gil."

Gil looked surprised. "No, I don't." He filled a water glass and shoved it toward Justin. "Drink up!"

Justin looked about again, fear on his thin face. There was no help forthcoming from any of the hardcases standing about him. Most of them were half drunk, or well on the way to being half drunk. There was a maliciousness showing on their faces, like small boys torturing a cat or dog. Maybe an otherwise dull evening might be enlivened. A man like Justin rated about level with a cat or dog, with maybe the dog having a mite more standing.

"Drink!" said Gil.

The little man picked up the glass and downed the strong spirits. Gil refilled the glass and shoved it toward Justin. A second time he emptied it. His face was flushed and his eyes were wide in his head.

"Once more," said Gil.

"Let me be, Rorkin," pleaded Justin.

Gil slowly and deliberately filled the glass until the liquor bulged over the rim. He looked at Justin and then at the glass. His meaning was plain enough.

"He's had enough, Gil," said the bartender. "You know what will happen to him when he gets home. His niece will raise hell with me."

"Shut up, Charley," said Gil. "Drink up, Justin."

Justin downed the liquor. A peculiar, spasmodic twitching came over him. He closed his eyes and then opened them, then he reached for the bottle, only to have Gil take it away from his clutching hand. "That's all for tonight, Justin," he said cheerfully.

Justin wiped his mouth with the back of a hand. "Give me a drink, Charley," he said. There was a note of desperation in his voice.

Gil looked Charley in the eye. Charley shook his head. "I want no trouble here, Justin," he said.

The little man stood there looking from Gil to Charley, then to the bottle and back again. He reached out a hand and Gil shook his head. "There ain't another saloon within twenty miles of here," said Justin slowly. "There ain't a bottle at the ranch. For God's sake, Gil!" His voice had a breaking quality in it as he finished.

"Get out," said Gil. "Go on home, Justin. You ain't a real drinking man. Go on home and dream about the Texas Rangers coming to buy you a drink. Go on now!"

Justin backed away to the middle of the bar. A half-empty glass of whisky stood there. He shot out a hand toward it but Gil Rorkin was too fast. A Colt leaped into his hand and the bullet reached the glass an inch ahead of Justin's fingertips, splattering glass and whisky against Justin's taut face. The smoke wreathed along the bar, filling the big room with its acrid stench.

"For God's sake, Gil," said Charley. "You had no cause to do that! You might have hit him!"

Justin stood there like a whipped pup, tail between his legs. Slowly he turned and walked toward the door, only to stagger and fall heavily. He lay still on the filthy floor as Gil Rorkin roared with laughter.

Buck got up and walked to the little man. He knelt beside him and turned the white face.

"Get away from him, Cleburne," said Gil.

Buck ignored Rorkin. He looked up at Charley. "Where does he live?" he asked.

"Five miles out on the road leading west at the crossroads. The Reeves place. Can't miss it. Mule Ear Peak's right behind it."

Gil emptied his glass. "I said to get away from him, Cleburne," he repeated.

Buck looked up at Rorkin. "This man is in bad shape."

"You a doctor?" sneered Gil.

Buck shook his head. "It doesn't take a doctor to see it."

"Maybe you want a little of what I gave him?"

It was then that Buck noted that Justin carried no belt gun. He quickly passed a hand over the coat pockets, feeling for a stingy gun, a sawed off Colt or derringer. The man was unarmed. Something clicked into place in Buck's mind.

"His buckboard is outside," said a man at the end of the bar.

Gil's eyes were staring fixedly at Buck. It reminded Buck of the first time he had seen Gil Rorkin back at the ranch. The hovering madness trying to get control of the weak-reined sanity; the insane, almost homicidal look. He had seen that look again on the shadowed road leading into Mexico from the isolated ford on the Rio Grande, when Gil Rorkin had started killing the wounded smugglers and the thrashing horses.

A tenseness filled the smoky room. All eyes were on Buck Terrell as he stood over the help-less little man named Justin, facing Gil Rorkin who killed as other men made love.

Some perverse quality in Buck Terrell held

him there. Something he seemed to sense, hinted at by Tod Logan, something he had begun to realize.

"Get away from that drunk," said Gil.

"I seem to remember something about your brother's orders," said Buck softly.

Gil's face worked. Buck readied himself for a split second draw. A minute dragged past like a snake with a broken spine. Gil's mouth opened and closed. His mad eyes stared into the icy gray ones of Buck Terrell and he did not like what he saw. "Get to hell out'a here," he said harshly.

Buck picked up Justin and turned his back on Gil. Even Gil Rorkin could never live down the stigma of shooting a man in the back; a man who was doing a good turn for a helpless one.

Buck carried the unconscious man to the buckboard and placed him in the back, atop several sacks of feed. There was a box of groceries in the buckboard and other odds and ends. Evidently Justin had been shopping and had stopped in the saloon for a few beers before starting home. Buck tethered his horse to the tailgate of the buckboard, unhitched the team, then drove slowly out of town. He looked back as he reached the crossroads. There was no sign of Gil Rorkin in the street.

Buck rolled a cigarette and lighted it. Cold sweat had soaked his shirt below his armpits. No man likes to face a mad dog. No man likes to be faced down in his own bailiwick, and Buck had surely faced down Gil Rorkin. It was something Rorkin would never forget. His warped mind would not allow an insult to his colossal ego. No, there would be no dealing with Gil Rorkin. Buck had always stood on quaking ground with the man and this night had made the situation far worse.

He watched the faint rays of the new moon touch some low peaks ahead of him. Peaks shaped like mule's ears were about five miles ahead. That was his immediate goal. After that he'd have to decide whether to return for Gil and take his chances of a bullet in the belly, or light a shuck for Ysleta and tell Dan Lynch his courage had failed before he had even got a faint clue as to the killers of the four Rangers.

He blew out a smoke ring and looked back at Justin. The little man lay sprawled on his back, mouth gaping open, flecked blood showing blackly against the drawn whiteness of his face. Buck would have to explain what had happened, hoping his niece, whoever she was, would understand.

The moon had lit the countryside with a wash of pale silver when he reached the side road that led up to the Reeves place, perched on a slope sheltered from the winds by the mule ear peaks. A mule bawled from a corral. The windmill was whirring steadily. Yellow rectangles of lamp-light showed against the dull background of the ranch house. A thin wreath of smoke hung over the buildings.

Buck turned up the road and halted at a Texas gate. He got down to open it.

"Who are you?" a woman called out from the porch of the house.

Buck looked up. "Name of Spade Cleburne," he said. "I've got Mister Justin here."

There was a moment's pause. "Come in then, Mister Cleburne."

It was as though she expected people to bring Justin home. The front door opened, silhouetting her against the light, then she vanished inside the house. Buck drove up to the porch and dropped to the ground. He picked Justin up like a sack of wheat and stepped up on the porch. The wind had partly closed the door. "Wait," she said from inside. She held the door back while Buck carried the limp man inside and as he passed her his left arm brushed against firm breasts. He did not dare look at her until he placed Justin on a couch and loosened the little man's collar and belt. Buck took off his sweaty Mex hat and turned to look at her and as he did so his breath drew in. She was young, hardly more than twenty years of age. Light brown hair was caught at the back of her neck by a bright ribbon. Clear hazel eyes looked fully into his and a soft-looking mouth spoke words he did not hear for a moment, so dazzled was he.

"Don't you understand?" she said. Her eyes narrowed. "You're not Mexican, are you?"

Buck was startled. He had been completely taken by her loveliness. He smiled, if you could call the creasing of his scarred, browned, and dusty face, a smile. "I'll admit I look a little rough," he said. "I'm a Texan born and bred, ma'am."

"I asked you where you found him."

"He was in the saloon at the Crossroads."

"Drunk?"

Buck hesitated. "Not exactly."

"I'm India Reeves. Carl Justin is my mother's brother."

Buck rubbed a dusty hand over his dusty face. "He was in bad shape," he said. "I thought I had better drive him home. I got my horse outside. I'll be leaving now."

She tilted her head to one side and studied him. "You don't look like a Good Samaritan," she said with a little smile that completely disarmed him. It was getting harder to leave by the minute. "Are you just passing through?"

"No. I'm from the Rorkin rancho."

Her eyes narrowed again and a frosty look came into them. "Oh," she said.

He smiled. "I see you know the Rorkin *corrida*."

"How long have you been with them?"

"A little while."

"I thought so. None of the others would have brought him home." She walked to her uncle and placed a hand on his sweat dewed forehead. "He can't drink strong spirits. A few beers are what I allow him. He's been so good about it. It has been over a year since he was brought home like this. How did it happen?"

Buck walked toward the door. "I'll be headin' back, Miss India," he said.

She turned and walked toward him. "Tell me," she said.

97

"It wasn't his doing. One of the boys forced him to drink."

"Forced him?"

"Well, he had been doing some drinking on his own."

"Who forced him, Mister Cleburne?"

There was no use in lying to those penetrating, though lovely eyes. "Gil Rorkin," said Buck.

Her face grew taut. "I could have almost guessed that," she said quietly. "Everyone knows about Uncle Carl. Most of them steer him out of the saloon after he's had a few drinks. Why did Gil do it?"

Buck shrugged. "They had a little disagreement. Gil carries two six-guns and it seems as though your uncle doesn't carry a gun, not even a hideout gun. Odd for a West Texan."

"He stopped carrying a gun some years ago," she said. "His drinking and gunplay didn't mix. He had learned his lesson."

"Too bad some others can't learn that same lesson."

She looked back at her uncle. "He never forgot he had been a Texas Ranger years ago. He didn't drink at all in those days. It was after that, after his wife died, that he began to drink, lost his star, self-respect and almost his life. My mother kept him away from drink as long as she was alive, but when she was gone it was no use. I was young then. It's been only in the past year or so I have been able to keep him away from complete drunkenness."

"What has Gil Rorkin against him?" he said.

Her eyes studied him. "Two things: Uncle Carl was a Ranger, as I told you. Not very long. He wasn't quite the type, but it was the highlight of his life. He never forgot it. It became somewhat of a joke around here some years ago. He's never been able to live it down."

"And the other thing?"

"Me," she said simply. "I can't stand Gil Rorkin. Gil sickens me. When my father was alive he stayed away from the place. For a time he almost drove us from this country. I think it was his brother who made him let us alone. Powers Rorkin doesn't want any trouble around here." She laughed without mirth. "Powers Rorkin has big ideas and he doesn't want local trouble to interfere with his grand plans."

"Grand plans?" queried Buck.

She nodded. "He's just as mad as Gil, though in a different way. Powers Rorkin is on a one way road, to complete power or sudden death."

"You're a very observant young lady."

She eyed him. "Enough to know that there is something different about you, Mister Cleburne. You look like the Rorkin *corrida* type, but there is something different about you. What is it?"

Buck actually felt uncomfortable beneath her clear, penetrating gaze. "I'll be leaving now," he said. He walked out on the porch and turned toward her. "Tell your uncle to keep away from Gil Rorkin. He might have been killed tonight."

She came out on the porch and looked west across the moonlighted country. "I suppose we should leave here. I'm all he has now. But I can't leave this country. It is my home."

"The Rorkins are like drought, or plague," said Buck. "They have power for a time and they pass on."

"The passing on is taking time."

He looked up at the mule ear peaks. "Perhaps it won't be much longer," he said enigmatically. "Good night, Miss India." He walked down the steps and untethered his horse from the buckboard.

"I almost believe you," she said.

He turned and looked at her. "Why do you

say that, Miss Reeves?" he quietly asked. He smiled that curious twisted smile of his.

She leaned against a post and looked down at this hard case of a man. "I said there was something different about you, Mister Cleburne. Why do you ride with Powers Rorkin? Who are you really?" she asked.

He grinned. "A fine question to ask a Texan in the Big Bend country, and you a West Texan born and bred."

"Who are you?" she insisted.

"The name is Spade Cleburne," he said. "No more and no less."

"It does have a West Texas ring to it," she said. "You'd better hurry, Mister Cleburne, your friends will be waiting to hear what happened when you brought Uncle Justin home."

He rubbed his scarred cheek and looked sideways up at her. It was pleasant standing there talking to her, but he knew it was only a fleeting moment, and when he left, he'd likely never see her again. "I'm not much of a bar hound," he said.

"You don't drink?"

He smiled a little. "I just said I wasn't much

of a 'bar hound', ma'am. The bottle has been a friend of mine for a good many years."

"A false friend," she said.

He led the horse a few steps from the buckboard. "Don't moralize, ma'am. I'm not in the mood for it this night."

"I didn't mean to offend you," she said quickly.

"No harm done, ma'am," he said cheerfully.

"Good night, Mister Cleburne," she said.

"The name is Spade, Miss India."

For a few seconds she studied him. "*Really?* Good night, then, Spade."

He swung up into the saddle and rode toward the gate. He looked back once and saw her there, seeing her slim shape silhouetted against the yellow lamplight streaming from the open door, and it seemed to Buck Terrell that a small part of his soul had somehow remained behind, lost to him forever, unless, perhaps, he might see her again, and again and again, for Miss India Reeves was one woman he would never be able to forget.

6

THE Rorkin rancho was dreaming in the last faint rays of the dying moon when Buck Terrell crossed the creek up the canyon and followed the bank of the water course toward the rancho buildings. He was alone. When he had returned to the *cantina*, he had learned that Gil Rorkin had left without waiting for Buck. It was just as well in a sense. Buck would have been hard put to keep his temper in check listening to Rorkin's jibes and brags. Still, it had been Powers Rorkin's orders that Buck stay with Gil and return with him to the rancho. Powers Rorkin liked to have his orders obeyed. He had built his tough *corrida*, small as it was, on the basis of discipline, no mean feat when dealing with men like Beckett, Logan, Anthony, Perez, and above all, Powers' brother Gil. It had been Gil who had forced the issue on the Mexican side of the Rio despite the fact that Moss Beckett was in charge. It had been Gil who had delayed in returning to the rancho. He had been doing a great deal of talking in the *cantina*. Beckett had told them to stay out of trouble, to be seen but to keep their mouths shut in case there were any repercussions from the raid on the smugglers. None of those orders had been obeyed by Gil Rorkin. Gil might get away with disobedience, but Buck was still on trial with the *corrida*. He had been ordered to side Gil by Beckett's instructions, based on Powers Rorkin's orders. If Gil had returned to the rancho he might have shot off his big mouth, incriminating Buck in the eyes of the *corrida*, and worse still, in the eyes of Powers Rorkin.

There were other men in the *corrida*, but those who had participated in the raid on the smugglers formed the hard core of it, the elite. Rorkin had at least six-to-ten more men, some of them with the small cattle herd he maintained as a front, others in the hills, while others came and went in the dark of the moon, after mysterious consultations with Rorkin, and once Buck had been sure he had heard a woman talking to Rorkin late at night, and later had seen two riders leave the rancho, one of them as slim as a boy, and quite possibly it was the woman he had heard speaking with Rorkin. Rorkin kept his plans to himself.

"Halt! Stand where you are!" the sharp challenge came out of the shadowy trees between Buck and the first ranch buildings.

"It's Cleburne," said Buck. He had recognized the flat voice of Cap Anthony.

"Where's Gil?"

Gil had *not* returned then. Six of one and half a dozen of another. Gil would have made trouble for Buck by talking if he had returned ahead of Buck. Now he had made trouble for Buck by disappearing from the *cantina* back at the Crossroads.

"Where's Gil?" demanded Anthony.

"I lost him somewhere," said Buck.

"Jesus God! You was told to stick with him and keep him out'a trouble."

"I ain't his goddamned nurse!" snarled Buck.

"No," a quiet voice said. "You're not." It was the voice of Powers Rorkin. "Come on in, Cleburne. I want to talk with you."

Buck slid from the saddle and led his horse toward the buildings. He saw the figure of Powers Rorkin walking ahead of him toward the small building Powers shared with his brother as quarters. As Buck looked about he saw the heavy figure of Tod Logan standing in the doorway of a building just across from Rorkin's quarters. Logan nodded his head to Buck but there was no expression on his flat face.

Rorkin lit the lamp on the table and turned to look at Buck. "What happened?" he asked.

Buck figured he might as well tell the truth. "We stopped at the Crossroads *cantina* yesterday evening, figuring to ride in here tonight or tomorrow morning. Gil was doing some drinking, but he wasn't drunk."

"And you?"

Buck waved a hand. "I drink, but I can handle it."

"That's what all of you say." Rorkin lit a cigar from the lamp. "Go on."

"Gil was doing some talking."

"About what?" snapped Rorkin.

Buck felt for the makings and began to fashion a cigarette as he spoke. "Fast draws," he said dryly. "The usual thing. A lot of talk about Hardin, Courtright, Ben Thompson and the rest of the fast guns."

"Comparing himself with them, eh?"

Buck nodded. "There was a little man in there. Name of Carl Justin. He mentioned something about Rangers coming in here to look for the men who murdered four Rangers in the past year or so. Gil didn't like his talk.

He made the man drink. He might just as well have gut shot him. Justin passed out. He was in bad shape. I took him home."

Rorkin eyed Buck through the smoke. "Why you?"

Buck shrugged. "I was tired of sitting around waiting for Gil to make up his mind to leave."

"Your orders were to stay with him!"

Buck lit his cigarette. "Look, Rorkin," he said quietly. "You say I saved your life back in the Sierra Vieja. You took me on here because I'm a fast gun, on the wrong side of the law. You sent me out with Beckett and the boys to do that little job on the south side of the Rio, which we did. Up until the time I had to ride herd on your little brother, I did my job. Right?"

Rorkin flushed. "Yes," he admitted.

Buck leaned forward. "Gil *is* a fast gun. One of the fastest I have ever seen. On that basis he's of value to you. But beyond his gun skill he's a damned fool, and I don't mind telling you so to your face."

Rorkin waved a hand. "I know how you feel. I know how the rest of them feel about him. I can't kick him out of the *corrida*, Cleburne. I agree. He's so convinced that his speed with his guns is the only answer, that he's forgotten everything else I've tried to teach him."

"He might have the lot of us killed some day."

"That's why I sent you along with him!"

Buck inspected his cigarette. "Maybe you should have sent someone else," he said softly. "He hates my guts."

Rorkin did not answer. He walked to a window and looked out toward the last dying rays of the new moon.

Buck knew the answer. Gil Rorkin hated the guts of every other member of the *corrida*, and the feeling was mutual. Gil Rorkin was the weak link in the chain. If Powers Rorkin was as hard a case as he acted, he would have gotten rid of his brother long ago. If Gil Rorkin was the weak link in the chain, his brother's misplaced loyalty to him was also another weak link.

Rorkin slapped a hand hard against the wall. "It was a clean sweep over there," he said, almost as though to himself. "Twenty thousand in gold! No witnesses. No repercussions because of the deaths of men who are just as outside the law as we are. By God, that's the way I like to do my business! No witnesses! That's the key!"

A cold feeling came over Buck. Four Rangers had paid the price of life for perhaps being witnesses to some of Rorkin's outlawry. "What next?" he asked. "Lay low for a time? Make plans for another raid?"

Rorkin turned slowly. "You know better than to ask me my plans! I'll tell you this, Cleburne: Twenty thousand in gold is nothing but a fly speck on what we'll reap one of these days! We'll use the twenty thousand as our bankroll. No more of this penny-ante stuff. We cashed in our six-guns for that smugglers' gold. Nice, neat deal, eh, Cleburne?"

Buck shrugged. "We could have handled the deal without bringing Sanchez into it," he said. He grinned evilly. "Hellsfire! The boys from the *corrida* didn't need those Mexes to help us." He dropped into a chair and shoved back his Mex hat.

Rorkin eyed him. "I thought it was a good plan," he said slowly. "Parado had fifteen men with him. Supposing he would have had thirty?"

"He didn't," said Buck flatly.

"How was I to know?"

Buck looked up at him. "You're the brains here, Mister Rorkin. You knew Parado was going to cross the Rio Grande that night. You knew he had that gold with him. With all that information, you should have *known* he had only fifteen men with him."

Rorkin's dark face tightened. "You're talking too big for your britches," he said hotly.

"No offense, Boss," said Buck placatingly. "By godfrey, you've got a good secret service working, but it could be better. There was no need to risk having Sanchez in on the deal. Supposing he had brought twenty or thirty men with him? Do you think *he* would have let us live after we lifted that gold from Parado?"

Rorkin wet his thin lips. "You've got a point there, Spade," he admitted.

"Another thing: If any of Parado's men, or Sanchez' men had escaped, they would have had the whole countryside roused up about us. Maybe they'd have to wait for a crack at us, but we're not so far from the Rio Grande that they couldn't cross the Rio in the dark of the moon and raid us here. It's been done many times in this country. Lucky for us that Parado *and* Sanchez were wiped out."

Rorkin leaned against the wall and relit his cigar. "Why?" he asked.

Buck looked up at him. "There may be a time when we'll have to pull leather across the Rio Grande a jump and a spit ahead of the Rangers. It'll pay us to have friends on the other side. You know as well as I do that all Mexes are related to each other like all the pretty girls in Georgia."

Rorkin studied Buck for a few minutes. "I took you on here because I needed fast guns, not fast brains. I'm the brains around here, Cleburne."

Buck shrugged. "Maybe I talk too much."

Rorkin shook his head. He grinned. "I've been hoping I'd find a man who can work out councils of war with me. Moss is a good tool. He does what he's told to do and does it well, but he can't think beyond his immediate orders. I hate to admit it, but Gil is of no help. The others, well, they do their jobs and they do them well." Rorkin paced back and forth. "The weight of making plans, and seeing that they're carried out is hell on one man."

Buck fashioned another cigarette. So far he had carried off his bluff. The job on the Mexican side of the river was over, with no

111

great loss to the United States or Mexico. About twenty outlaws had died, and neither of the two countries would mourn their loss. The twenty thousand was outlaw money, its original source being unknown. It was no longer of any concern to Buck. It was the secretive plan of Rorkin's that was interesting to him. If it was as big as Rorkin hinted it was, it must be big indeed, and something which Dan Lynch would be mightily interested in, but until Buck had an inkling of what it was he must still play his cards close to his belly and keep his own counsel.

"Damn Gil anyway!" burst out Rorkin with a suddenness that startled Buck. He looked quickly at Buck. "You too tired to go back with me?"

Buck shrugged. "I'll go if you want me to."

"Tell Tod to saddle my horse and get a fresh one for you. We'll leave in twenty minutes."

Buck walked outside. He was a little tired, but it was no time to hold back on anything that might help him in his mission. Rorkin was worried about some of his information getting out. Gil had a big mouth. Therefore Rorkin had to find his brother to make sure he wasn't talking. If he *did* talk, Buck aimed to be around him.

"The Boss wants his horse saddled, Logan," said Buck. "Get me a fresh one too. I'm going to change into fresh clothing."

Tod nodded. "Where's the Kid?" he asked.

"*Quien sabe?*"

"I thought Rorkin would be raising hell with you for coming back without him. You must'a had a good story."

Buck shrugged. "It was the truth," he said. He grinned. "For once in my life telling the truth paid off."

Tod shoved back his hat. "Rorkin ought to get rid of him," he said quietly. He glanced at Buck. "Me and the rest of the boys feel that Gil is a danger to us all."

"Sure he is, but what do you aim to do about it?"

Tod smiled enigmatically. "We'll see," he said. He walked off toward the corrals.

Buck went to his room and changed quickly. As he buckled his gun belt he had a feeling he was being watched. He turned quickly. Blas Perez stood in the doorway watching Buck. There was something inhuman about the man. For all his weight and corded muscles, he walked like a cat. "The *patron* is waiting," he

113

said in his metallic voice. "Where do you look for the Kid?"

Buck shrugged. "The Crossroads, I suppose."

"He will not be there."

"So?"

What passed for a smile crossed the dark, hard face. "If he is not there, try Tres Jacales, five miles south of the Crossroads."

Buck picked up his jacket and shrugged into it. "Gambling place?" he said.

"No. A place of women. The Kid likes his women as well as he does the sight and smell of blood. But, he never goes after the women unless he is very drunk."

Buck walked to the door and put out the lamp in passing. Blas stepped outside. "The *patron* is worried about him, eh?"

"Yes."

Blas watched Buck walk toward the front of the building. His dark eyes narrowed. The thought occurred to him again, as it had a number of other times, that he had known Buck from somewhere else, but the time and place was lost in memory.

Buck and Rorkin rode up the valley in the gathering darkness after the moon had vanished to the west. They left the isolated valley and rode along a saddleback ridge, then between two humped peaks, until they reached the faint trail that led into the valley that held the Crossroads, and the Reeves' ranch. There were few other places of habitation in that country. Buck knew well enough why Rorkin had established his headquarters in that area. There were few eyes to see and few ears to hear anything that was going on, and the few people that lived there knew better than to shoot off their mouths. The memories of four dead Rangers was enough to gag any mouth. If these men dared to kill Rangers, they'd kill anyone else who stood in their way, and the truth was that the Rangers had done nothing to date to bring in the killers of Frank Terrell, Francisco Armenderiz, Cooke Durkee and Kelly Ledbetter. Four graves to Boot Hill and not a single arrest of the men who had done the cold-blooded killings.

Buck rolled a cigarette and lit it. He glanced at Rorkin. "Heard a rumor at the Crossroads," he said casually.

"So?" said Rorkin.

"Heard it said a Ranger was seen near Tres Jacales."

Rorkin looked quickly at him. "Tres Jacales?"

"I'm pretty sure that's the place."

Rorkin shifted in his saddle. "What do you know about Tres Jacales?"

"Nothing."

Rorkin nodded. "Let's speed it up," he said.

"Where we headin', Boss?" asked Buck.

"Tres Jacales," said Rorkin.

They rode down toward the rutted road that led past the Reeves place. The house was dark when they passed it. Powers Rorkin glanced at it. "I've been damned suspicious of that bunch," he said.

"You mean Carl Justin?"

Rorkin shook his head. "Justin is a drunkard," he said. "Still thinking he's a Ranger. No, he's too scared to open his mouth. It's that woman."

"India Reeves."

"Yes." Rorkin looked at Buck. "You met her?"

Buck grinned. "Couldn't hardly help doing that. Nice little filly."

Rorkin spat. "Hard as a diamond inside," he said. "Gil had ideas about her for a long time. I finally had to tell him to leave her alone. I don't give a damn about her. It's about time some real man bedded her and taught her a lesson or two, but I didn't want Gil doing too much talking around her. Now, if it was a man running that place, he'd have been taught his lesson, but Texans don't like a nice woman kicked around. They'll stand for a lot, but nothing like that. I can't afford to have trouble from the people who live around here."

"Who was going to kick her around?"

Rorkin was silent for a few minutes. "You've evidently never seen Gil around a woman when he's been drinking," he said and there was no need to say more. He had painted a pretty good picture in that one sentence.

The Crossroads was blacked out when they rode through it. Not a light showed. Not a horse was tethered to a hitching rack. Not a man was to be seen. Nothing but the steady thudding of the hoofs on the hard road. Tres Jacales was five miles south of the Crossroads.

They heard the gunfire when they were within half a mile of Tres Jacales, carried on the predawn wind. Rorkin cursed savagely and spurred his horse toward the sound of the shooting. He drew rein on a rise overlooking the area. Buck drew up beside him. Below them, hardly distinguishable in the darkness, was a cluster of buildings. Even as they looked a gun spoke, sparking orange-red flame from a window of one of the larger buildings.

The shot was answered from a motte of trees beyond the rutted road. Then it was silent again.

Powers Rorkin shoved back his hat. "It's Gil, I'm sure of it," he said.

"Which one? In the building or amongst the trees?"

Rorkin shrugged.

"We can wait until dawn to see," suggested Buck.

"No!" snapped Rorkin. "That damned fool is roaring drunk by now. What if that's a Ranger he's fighting with?"

Buck shrugged. "So it's a Ranger," he said casually. "Hell! Haven't your boys taken care of Rangers before this time?"

Rorkin seemed to stiffen a little. He slowly turned his head and stared at Buck with unblinking eyes. "Who told you that?" he said in a low voice.

Buck shrugged again. "Maybe I just had the idea," he said.

Rorkin bent his head forward. "From where, Cleburne? *From where . . . ?*" he insisted.

Buck took his cigarette from his mouth and snuffed it out against a boot. "I can't seem to remember," he said vaguely.

"Was it Gil?" demanded Rorkin.

Buck scratched the side of his neck and shook his head. "It just don't come back to me, Boss. I can't remember."

Rorkin's left hand shot out and gripped Buck by the right wrist. "Yes you can, Cleburne!" he rasped.

A gun cracked flatly from below them and the orange-red flash flicked out and was gone while the echo of the shot carried across the rolling country. Rorkin slowly released his hold on Buck's wrist. "I've got to get Gil out of this mess," he said quietly.

Buck looked sideways at him. "Let me make a scout down there," he suggested. "We've got to get the lay of the land and find out who's doing all the shooting."

"Go ahead. Don't be seen. I'm no good at that sort of thing, Spade." Rorkin seemed to have forgotten his tense questioning of Buck about the Ranger killings.

Buck swung down from the saddle and

removed his spurs. He hung his hat on the saddle horn by the *barbiquejo* chin strap and then walked softly down the long slope to vanish into a draw that would give him cover until he got nearer the house. It had been a close thing up there on the ridge. Powers Rorkin was almighty sensitive about those Ranger killings. There was one thing Buck knew that Powers Rorkin didn't know—the Texas Rangers were a helluva lot more sensitive about Ranger killings than Powers Rorkin could ever be.

7

BUCK TERRELL crawled along an eroded adobe wall and peered around the end of it. He was fifty feet from the rear of the building from which the gunfire was coming. One shot had been fired from the building as he had worked his way toward it. Not a sound came from any of the other buildings. It seemed to be a two man battle, but which one of the two was Gil Rorkin if it was indeed him at all? Powers Rorkin wasn't so stupid. He had let Buck take the risks to find out what was going on.

Buck darted across the rear of the building. A gun flashed in the motte and the slug sang thinly from the top of the adobe wall. The sharpshooter in the motte had eyes like a cat. Buck flattened himself against the rear wall and edge toward a door. The darkness was thick and as yet there was no sign of the false dawn. Buck eased his Colt in its sheath and tried the door. It swung open a little at his touch. He pushed it open and eased inside. An unmistakable odor came to him. The mingled aura of sweat, cheap perfume and women. What was it Blas Perez had said? "If he is not there, try Tres Jacales, five miles south of the Crossroads. A place of women. The Kid likes his women as well as he does the smell and sight of blood. But, he never goes after the women unless he is very drunk."

Buck peered into the thick and velvety darkness. He felt his way forward and found another door. He eased it open and peered into thick darkness again. A muffled shot sounded from the front of the building. Buck padded forward and his knees struck something soft and he could not keep himself from pitching forward atop something warm and soft. There was a startled outcry from beneath him, the voice of a woman. He felt bare arms against his face. "Quiet," he hissed.

"For the love of God!" she said. "Who is it? Gilberto?"

"No," he said. "A friend of Gilberto's. Spade Cleburne."

"I am Theresa. I do not know you. I know the others. Cap, Tod, Moss, Cuchillo, all of them. Sometimes some of them come here."

He felt a bare arm slide around his neck and

she drew him close, seeking his lips with hers. The ripe odor of whisky and woman flooded his nostrils. He could feel full, unhampered breasts pushing against his chest. By godfrey, she was as naked as a jaybird! He pushed her back and stood up. "Later," he said. He couldn't help but grin. Business came first with Theresa, even if two men were trying to let out a little life's blood within rock throwing distance of her. "I have to see Gilberto."

She sat up in the bed. "He is very drunk and loco in the head. Do not walk in there. He will shoot and ask questions later."

He passed a hand across her thick hair. "Who is he fighting with?"

"There was a shooting earlier this evening. A man was killed. A Ranger came. It is he who is shooting at Gil."

An icy feeling came over Buck. He had called the shot without realizing it by telling Powers Rorkin a tall tale about a Ranger supposedly being seen at Tres Jacales. "Who was killed?" asked Buck.

"*Quien sabe?* He was in this place and wanted to stay with me. We were drinking when Gilberto arrived. There was an argument.

The other girls left. They know better than to stay here when Gilberto arrives."

"Why didn't you leave?"

There was a pause. "I love him," she said in a low voice. "No matter what he does to me, I love him. He is very bad at times. There are bruises still on my body from the last time."

"Go on," said Buck, sickened at what she had mentioned.

"This other man was very drunk. He would not leave. Gilberto threw him out. There was shooting."

"Who drew first?"

Again a silence. "I did not see," she said cagily.

"And?"

"Gilberto would not leave after he killed the man. Someone must have gone for a Ranger. He came to the house to get Gilberto. Gilberto opened fire. That is all I know."

"Are there any others around?"

"Not in this house. I was afraid to leave after the shooting started."

Too damned drunk, thought Buck. He walked to the door that led into the next room. "What is in there?" he asked.

"A bar. Tables and chairs." She laughed. "And Gilberto, of course."

He stood there in the darkness, Colt in hand, wondering what to do. It was too early in the game to have another Ranger butt in, and wherever this particular Ranger had come from, he damned likely didn't know that Buck was working undercover within the Rorkin *corrida*. All he knew was that a man had been killed. As a Ranger it was his job to bring in the killer. It was as simple as that.

"Go on in," suggested Theresa. "Maybe he won't shoot." She laughed again as she began to dress.

"Will he shoot at you?"

"I do not think so."

"Then go in and tell him Spade Cleburne is here and that his brother is waiting out on the ridge."

She was silent for a moment. "His brother?" she said in a low, shaken voice.

"You heard me, *chiquita*."

"Mother of God! I am afraid of that one even more than of Gilberto. He has eyes like the devil."

"Well, if you don't go in and tell Gilberto I

am here, I'll have to go and get his brother to talk to him."

She was off the bed in an instant, to walk past Buck and poke her head around the edge of the door. "Gilberto!" she called.

A gun cracked flatly in the room. The acrid stench of burnt gun powder came to Buck.

"Gilberto!" she cried.

"What the hell you want, *puta!*" he said thickly. "I tol' you to keep an eye ona back door."

"There is a friend to see you."

Glass grated on the floor. Gil cursed in a low voice. Boots scraped on the sanded floor. "Friend?" said Gil suspiciously. "Got no friends but my six-guns."

"It's Spade Cleburne, Gil," said Buck. He cautiously stepped to one side.

"Where ahell did yuh go?" blurted Gil.

"You were gone when I came back."

"Ahell I was!"

Damn him, thought Buck, he's looped to the ears. "Listen, Gil," he said. "Your brother came back with me. He's waiting up on the ridge. He's fractious, I tell you!"

"What the hell does he want me to do? They's a Ranger out there on the peck and he's ain't aimin' to leave until he gets me or I get him."

Buck raised his head. "You worried?" he said.

Gil laughed. "Hell," he said. "I've tallied a few of 'em before this time."

"Your brother doesn't want any trouble now."

Gil hesitated. "Come on in," he said.

Buck walked into the smoke-filled room. He held his Colt at waist level, thumb on hammer, ready to shoot and shoot fast if the whisky fool took it into his *cabeza* to start shooting.

"Drink?" said Gil. "Bar's over there. Ona house, *hombre*." He laughed thickly.

Buck walked to the dimly seen bar and poured a drink. He needed it. "How long do you aim to sit here shooting at that Ranger?" he asked.

"Long's I damned well feel like it."

"With a six-gun?"

"You got any better ideas?"

Buck wiped his mouth. "So happens I have."

"Such as?"

"I'll leave and try to get around behind him."

"You ain't got the guts to kill a Ranger!"

"I wasn't figgerin' on killin' him, Gil."

127

"That's the only way *we* handle 'em," said Gil softly.

"Too dangerous," said Buck. "Powers don't want it."

"Screw Powers!"

"You tell him that," said Buck. "It ain't up to me to do it."

Gil suddenly turned. "That tin-star bastard ain't shooting," he said suspiciously.

Buck tilted his head to one side. It was very quiet. It was *too* quiet. He started toward the front door of the house. The door slammed toward him as he reached it and it drove him back against the wall, gasping for breath, his six-gun clattering on the floor. A short, chunky figure charged in. Gil fired and missed. In the flash of the gun Buck saw a star pinned to the vest of the intruder. He was a Ranger all right! Buck thrust out a leg. The Ranger tripped and went sprawling across the floor, hitting Gil just above the knees and slamming him back across a chair. His gun thudded against the floor.

There was no time to waste. Buck made a split second decision. He snatched up his gun and darted toward Gil. He swung the heavy gun and the long barrel caught the drunk just above the ear, hurling him to the floor for the long count. Buck stepped on the Ranger's gun wrist and covered his mouth with his left hand. "For Christ's sake," he said in a low voice. "Listen and listen well! I'm Terrell, working undercover in the Rorkin *corrida*. Powers Rorkin is outside somewhere. I can't have you butting in here like this. You understand?"

The man stared at him. He tried to talk around Buck's hand. Buck removed it from the Ranger's mouth. "I knew you were working in the Big Bend country," he said. "I'm Fred Carpenter. Jesus God, Terrell, I didn't know you were around here. All I did was get a call about a man being killed here at Tres Jacales. Who is this bastard?"

"Gil Rorkin."

"Oh my God! How do we get out of this one?"

Buck dragged him to his feet. He hurried to the front door. A body lay sprawled in the street. It was the man Gil had killed. Buck turned to Carpenter. "Give me your star," he said.

"Can't do that," said Carpenter.

Buck ripped it from the man's vest. "No time to argue," he said. He walked outside, looked up and down the dark street, then pinned the

Ranger star to the man's shirt. He dragged the body close to the front of the house. He ran around to the back and into the back door. He dimly saw Theresa standing with her back to him. She turned as he walked in and a hard fist caught her on the point of the jaw. He caught her before she fell and dropped her on the bed. He walked into the next room. "Get the hell out of here," he said. "Send a message to Lynch that I haven't gathered enough evidence yet to make a move."

"How the hell do you figure on getting out of this mess? They'll get wise to you."

"Not if you get out of here right now. Pull leather, Ranger!"

Carpenter wasted no time. He left the building and was gone out of sight in seconds.

Buck knelt beside Gil. The man was still unconscious. He dragged him outside and went back for Theresa to carry her to Gil. He dragged the stranger's body into the house. He smashed a lamp and threw a burning match into the pool of oil. It flared up instantly and greedily began to lick at the dry wood. Buck swiftly searched the body. He took the wallet and hat, then ran out the back way. There was no sign of Powers Rorkin. Buck ran across the

130

street and threw the wallet into a gully. He scaled the hat further up the gully and then ran back to the house. Firelight was showing through the windows and the open doorway. Hooves thudded on the hard street at the edge of the *placita*. It was Powers Rorkin with the two horses. Buck dragged Gil across the street and then went back for Theresa. The flames were roaring within the front room of the house. No one would walk in there now.

A woman screamed further up the street. A man shouted. Doors slammed open. A dog barked. Fat sparks drifted from the burning house and settled on a roof. Glass shattered from the intense heat within the room.

"What the hell happened?" said Powers Rorkin.

Buck wearily wiped his face. "The Ranger rushed the house when I got in there," he said. "Flattened Gil. He turned on me."

"Yes?"

Buck looked up at him. "He's still in there," he said.

Rorkin whistled softly. "Not another one?" he said, as though to himself.

Buck leaned back against the wall. The *placita* was fully lighted by the roaring fire.

Faint gray light was showing in the eastern skies.

Powers Rorkin dismounted and shoved back his hat. "Anyone see you kill him?" he said.

"Gil and the whore were both unconscious," said Buck.

"No one else?"

"No."

Rorkin's hard eyes flicked up and down the street. "I don't like this," he said. "Why was the Ranger after Gil?"

"It seems there was a shooting."

"Another one?"

Buck nodded. "Some *hombre* who tangled with Gil about Theresa."

"Gil didn't get shot?"

"No." Buck wet his dry lips and felt for the makings. He had to take his gamble now. If anyone knew for sure that the stranger had been shot to death, then Buck might be up to his neck in a privy and no gold watch at the bottom of it.

"Where is the other man? The one who was shot?"

Buck shrugged. "*Quien sabe?*" Buck fashioned a quirly and lit it. He glanced toward the gully where he had planted the hat and the wallet. "Took off maybe," he added.

Rorkin rubbed his jaw, moodily eyeing the devouring flames. "It isn't like Gil to miss," he said.

"He was pretty damned drunk when I saw him."

"Yeh," said Rorkin thoughtfully. "The girl. What does she know?"

Buck shrugged. "She had a snootful herself."

Rorkin smashed a fist into his other palm. "By God," he said in a low, hard voice, "I can't afford any trouble right now. It's too close to the time."

Buck blew out a smoke ring. Theresa had not seen the actual shooting, or at least she had *said* she had not. If she knew for certain the stranger had been killed, there would be a hell of a lot of explaining for Buck to do. He'd never talk his way out of that. If she had not seen the shooting, there might have been others in the *placita* who had. One of them had gone for the Ranger. He would probably know if the man had died, unless he had been so afraid of Gil Rorkin that he had not closely examined the body.

The sweetish sickening odor of burning

human flesh drifted across the smoky street. The false dawn was lighting the eastern sky beyond the mountains. The few people who lived in the *placita* had left the street and gone into their houses. They wanted nothing to do with the hard-eyed Yanqui men who stood there in that street of sudden death. In the center of the street, in front of the burning building was a black stain of blood where the stranger had died.

"Go look for the man Gil shot," said Rorkin suddenly. He slanted his flat green eyes at Buck. "If you find him, and he's still alive, you know what to do."

Buck nodded. He flipped his cigarette onto the street and walked past the gully. He rounded the corner of a big adobe and rolled another cigarette. He lit it, looking toward the rough country behind the *placita*. A man could easily lose himself in there. He poked about in the brush and amidst the trees, making a great show of searching. He topped a low ridge and saw a windmill and full water tank. Some of the water had overflowed. Hoof marks showed in the thin mud. Fred Carpenter must have kept his horse there while he had been trying to pry Gil Rorkin out of the besieged house. The tracks vanished on harder ground. Buck walked back toward the gully. He saw Powers Rorkin down on one knee examining something. It was the hat of the stranger. He looked up at Buck as Buck approached.

"Hoof marks up there," said Buck. "Vanished on hard ground."

"I found a hat and wallet here," said Rorkin. He stood up. "He's got too good a lead to chase after him now."

"Why worry about him? It's the Ranger's death that will cause trouble."

Rorkin nodded. "None of these people will talk. They better not! It's only Theresa who bothers me. She has a big mouth. A few drinks and she's liable to spill her guts." Rorkin walked toward the street.

Gil was seated on the street with his back against a wall, holding his throbbing head in his hands. There was no sign of Theresa. Powers Rorkin stopped in front of his brother and stood there looking down at him. "Are you ready to come with us?" he asked coldly.

"Let me alone, Powers," snarled Gil.

"Get up, you damned fool!"

Gil got slowly to his feet. His eyes were bloodshot and he stared dully at his brother.

"Go on," he said thickly. "Chew me out! Go ahead!"

"Do you know a Ranger died here this morning?"

"So?"

"By God, Gil! We can't afford to take any chances!"

"I didn't kill *him*. It was some other *hombre* I killed."

"You didn't kill *him* either! He got away!"

Gil's eyes narrowed. Buck eased away a little from the two of them and hooked his right thumb over his gun belt, just above his Colt. Gil passed a shaky hand across his face. "I was sure I got the drop on him," he said uncertainly.

"Looks like you didn't. Looks like that Ranger had the drop on you too. If it hadn't been for Cleburne here, he would have had you cold."

Gil's eyes narrowed again. He glanced suspiciously at Buck. The liquor had dulled his senses, and he wasn't sure of himself. "I ain't so sure that Ranger got me," he said slowly.

"You ain't sure of *anything!*" rapped out Powers.

"Any orders, Boss?" asked Buck quickly.

136

The fire had gutted the interior of the house by now and was dying out, flickering over charred wood. In the center of the front room was the charred corpse of the man Gil had killed.

"Find that woman!"

Gil looked dully at Powers. "What for?" he asked.

"She's going with us. We can't afford to have her talk."

"You won't get her out of here."

"She'll go if you say you want to marry her. Live with her anyway."

"To hell with that!"

Powers gripped Gil by the shirt front. "You want her to talk, you idiot!"

"It wasn't me who killed the Ranger. It was Cleburne."

"Yeh! To save *your* life!" snapped Powers.

Buck walked along the street. He reached the end house and rapped on the door. An old woman opened it. "Is Theresa here?" asked Buck.

The woman nodded. She opened the door and stepped to one side. Theresa sat on a couch, moodily examining her bruises. "What do you want?" she said. She was still pretty drunk.

137

"Gil Rorkin wants you to ride with us."

"To hell with him!"

The woman had vanished into the dark interior of the house. Buck leaned against the wall. "You said you loved him," he said casually.

She eyed him suspiciously. "What is that to you?"

Buck shrugged. "This is your chance, *chiquita*," he said carelessly. "It means nothing to me."

She hesitated. "Does he mean it?"

"He asked for you," he said.

She got up and draped a shawl about her bare shoulders. "I do not believe it," she said.

"Go ask him," said Buck. He watched her wriggle through the doorway. She had a soft spot in her pretty head for Gil Rorkin, God help her.

Powers Rorkin came out of the still-burning house as Buck came up the street. Rorkin was tossing something small back and forth in his gloved hands, as though it was hot. He held it up so that Buck might see it. It was the fire-blackened Texas Ranger star Buck had pinned on the dead stranger's shirt. Beyond Powers, Gil was talking to Theresa, smiling in spite of the hell's pounding that must be going on within his whisky soaked brain and because of the buffaloing given him by Buck. Theresa was all aglow, looking up into Gil's handsome face. She was rapidly nodding her head. Gil slid an arm about her waist and walked with her to where his horse was tethered to a hitching rail. He swung up into the saddle and then pulled her up in front of him, while he made free with his hands within her clothing. The little fool of a woman squealed in rapture.

It was a puzzler to Buck. He shaped a cigarette as he walked to get his horse and that of Powers Rorkin. He lit it, glancing back toward Gil and Theresa. Rorkin walked to where Buck was waiting with the horses. Rorkin looked sourly at the burning house. "Cost me a hundred in gold to stopper up the mouths around here," he said. "They agreed to get rid of the corpse." He watched Gil riding slowly along the road with the woman on the saddle with him. "It'll take a little more time and care with her," he added.

Buck looked sideways at the outlaw. There was something etched on Rorkin's face; something that Buck could not fathom, but he knew well enough it boded no good for the woman Theresa.

The sun was tipping the eastern range as they rode to the top of the ridge. Low behind them a wraith of bluish smoke still hung in the windless air. Buck looked back down the ridge. Already some of the men of the *placita* were lifting the corpse into a *carreta*. The *carreta* creaked down the smoke filled street. In a little while the dead stranger, thought to be a Texas Ranger, would be buried forever in an unmarked grave.

8

THE Rorkin *corrida*, with the exception of Gil Rorkin, who, with his bride-to-be Theresa, had left the rancho two days before to travel north to get married, was gathered in the big main room of the large adobe on the Rorkin rancho. Powers Rorkin had moved up his plans. Gil had nearly jeopardized everything by his wild and undisciplined conduct. It was better that he was out of the way, with a bag of the smuggler's gold and Theresa to keep him busy until things quieted down.

Powers Rorkin stood beside the fireplace, a thin cigar in his mouth, eyeing his group of hardcases. "We've got three days to work out the deal," he said. "No *more* and no *less*. After we spring this one we scatter. Some of you head for Mexican Coahuila. Some of you into East Texas. In six months or so we'll get together again."

"Six months?" said Tod Logan. "What do we live on?"

Rorkin blew a smoke ring. "Don't worry about that," he said. "With the twenty thousand we took across the Rio, plus the profits from the new job, we can live like kings."

Blas Perez was sharpening his *cuchillo*. "What is the deal, *Patron?*"

Rorkin smiled thinly. "The railroad has a branch line running into the mines at Lone Hills. A bullion train goes in every few months. Nonscheduled. No one but the train crew and the line officials, as well as the manager of the mines, knows which train is the bullion train. I have information to that effect."

Moss Beckett shook his head. "Bullion is hell to carry," he said, "if there's too much of it." He cocked an eye at Powers.

"We're not interested in the bullion," said Powers. "The miners haven't been paid off for three months. The next trip of the train carries *in* the payroll. They usually don't handle it this way, but the miners have been getting ugly about not being paid. There was some financial trouble with the company, but it has been straightened out now. The payroll, as well as a big sum of expense money, is due in there in three days. Cash is a hell of a lot easier to handle than bullion."

"How much?" said Cap Anthony.

Powers smiled again. "Over sixty thousand, *amigos*."

"I don't believe it!" said Tod Logan.

"Tell them, Blas," said Rorkin.

Cuchillo sheathed his thin-bladed knife. "They have been running twenty-four hour shifts," he said quietly. "Many of my people from Coahuila are working there. More than I have ever seen. The present mines are being worked to capacity. They are sinking new shafts. It is like the huge ant hill there." He looked at Rorkin. "I did not know we were ready for this job, *Patron*."

"I said we had three days to work it out. We can't wait any longer. The next payroll will be one-third this size."

"You're sure of the amount?" said Cap.

"You can bet on it," said Rorkin.

"Go ahead with the details," said Moss Beckett.

"The train slows down at Estacado," said Rorkin, "because of the grade there, then hasn't enough time and distance to get up enough speed to get through Tornillo Canyon except at a snail's pace. It will be about dusk when it enters the canyon. We can hit it at the other

143

end of the canyon where the walls narrow, leaving just about enough room for it to get through. We can drop atop the cars. Some of us can get to the engine and have it stopped. The others can take care of the payroll car. The whole job shouldn't take more than half an hour to forty-five minutes."

"What about the payroll guards?" asked Tod.

"They can't get at us if we're on top of the car," said Rorkin.

"And we can't get at them," said Cap Anthony.

"Don't worry about that," said Rorkin. "We can blow the roof off that damned car. I've got blasting powder and Moss knows how to use it."

"What about the noise?" said Blas.

"Who's around to hear it but the train crew and the payroll guards?" said Rorkin.

"What happens after we lift the payroll?" asked Tod.

"We split up, like I said," answered Rorkin. "Choose your own partners. Only two men to travel together. In six months we can meet in say, Juarez, or Piedras Negras on the Mex side of the Rio."

Cap leaned back in his chair and eyed Rorkin. "Who takes care of the loot?" he said.

"We can cache it," said Rorkin. "When things cool down we can get it."

"Yeh?" said Cap softly. "Does that include the twenty thousand we lifted across the Rio?"

Rorkin frowned a little. "Of course!"

"We all cache it together?"

Rorkin cut a hand through the air. "Too dangerous."

Cap nodded. "I see. Who caches it then?"

"Me, of course."

"Of course," said Cap dryly. "You and your brother, eh, Mister Rorkin?"

It was very quiet in the big room. Buck Terrell blew a smoke ring and watched it drift toward an open window.

"What do you mean by that?" said Rorkin quietly.

"Eighty thousand dollars," said Cap. He looked at Tod Logan. "You travelin' with me, *amigo?*"

"Keno."

Cap looked at Moss Beckett. "Who'll side you?"

"Cuchillo," said Beckett.

145

Cap's colorless eyes shifted to Rorkin. "You ride with Cleburne?"

Rorkin nodded. Buck could hardly hide the surprise in his eyes. This was something Buck had never anticipated.

"What about Gil?" said Cap.

"He'll meet me and Spade here, over in Mexico," said Rorkin.

"Very neat," said Cap. He picked up a deck of cards and riffled them in his lean hands. "Why can't we split up the loot after we raid the train? Each party caches its own share."

"No go," said Rorkin.

"It's *ours* ain't it, Rorkin?" said Cap quietly.

The sound of the cards seemed loud in the room. Tod Logan coughed. Moss Beckett shifted his feet.

"Well, ain't it?" persisted Cap.

"I thought I was the boss here," said Rorkin.

"I didn't say you wasn't," said Cap.

The man was either extremely courageous or an outright idiot, thought Buck.

"Then I make the plans," said Rorkin flatly.

Cap smiled thinly. "Sure, you *make* the plans. But you don't get away with the loot to let the rest of us sit on our asses waiting to hear from you in six months now."

"You think you won't, eh?" said Rorkin coldly.

Cap waved a hand. "Another thing: Is Gil in on this deal?"

"Of course he is!"

Cap cocked a questioning eye at Rorkin. "I mean, does *he* raid the train with us?"

"He isn't here," said Rorkin.

"But he shares with the rest of us, doesn't he?" questioned Cap.

It was quiet again. Every man in that room knew what Cap was thinking. Gil was up north somewhere, marrying his Mexican inamorata, sleeping in a soft bed, boozing it up, while the rest of them, including his own brother, would risk their lives to gain the payroll.

"It's better that he isn't here," said Rorkin.

Cap nodded. "That's what I was thinkin'. But why? Because he boozed it up at the Crossroads, causing trouble. Then he gets in a mess at Tres Jacales. Supposing the Rangers find out one of their boys, *another* of their boys, was killed at Tres Jacales?"

"Gil didn't kill the Ranger!" snapped Rorkin.

"No, he didn't," agreed Tod Logan. "It was Cleburne who done it, but *why* did he have to do it? I'll tell you! Because Gil caused the

Ranger to be there, that's why! Now how do we know the Rangers ain't poking around looking for another one of their boys that was killed in this country? Five Rangers, Rorkin! Five goddamned Rangers get killed around here and us sitting on top of the deal waiting for them to close in on us like we're rats in a trap!"

"We ain't caught yet," growled Beckett.

Buck rolled a fresh cigarette. Gil Rorkin had caused a lot of friction amongst the members of the *corrida*. It was obvious that Tod Logan and Cap Anthony hated Gil's guts. They were siding each other. How did the others stand? Beckett would side Powers Rorkin. Blas Perez would pair off with Beckett when the raid was over. He was probably a Rorkin man. Buck lit up. He had known all along the weak link in the *corrida* was Gil. Only Powers' loyalty to his brother, misplaced as it was, kept the vicious Gil in the *corrida*.

Cap stood up. "I ain't giving trouble, Boss," he said, "but we feel if Gil ain't here, he don't share in the loot from the raid. He gets his share from the raid across the Rio, which is fair enough, but he either rides with us on the raid, or he gets cut out of his share."

"I thought I was the leader here," said Rorkin.

"You can't force us to accept Gil as a sharer in this deal," said Tod Logan.

"*I* can," said a well known voice from the open window.

Cap Anthony's expression didn't change, but Tod Logan paled a little beneath his tan. He swiveled his flat black eyes toward the window. A leg was thrust into the room, followed by the rest of Gil Rorkin. His face was taut and hard and his eyes did not blink. "I've heard the whole deal," he said in a low voice. "I aimed to come back and take my part. I never intended to let you *hombres* do the dirty work and leave me out of it."

"Where's Theresa?" asked Powers Rorkin.

"Never mind," said his brother shortly.

Buck took his cigarette from his mouth. There was something in the cold, mad eyes of Gil Rorkin that sent a chill creeping across his flesh.

Powers looked closely at his brother. "I don't want that woman to talk."

"She won't," said Gil. He grinned faintly.

"She's his bride," said Tod Logan. He

149

grinned too. "Helluva way to spend a honeymoon, ain't it, Cap?"

"Yeh," said Cap dryly. He never took his eyes off Gil.

Gil's head swiveled. "Shut up, you two," he said thinly. "You've done enough talking for tonight."

"Where is Theresa?" asked Powers Rorkin again.

There was no need for Gil to answer. The answer was plain enough to see on his satanic face.

"Jesus God," said Moss Beckett softly. "He done her in too!"

"She fell off a damned hoss," said Gil casually. "She was swilling aguardiente like it was sarsaparilla. Broke her pretty little neck like a damned matchstick." He rolled his eyes sorrowfully.

"I'll bet," said Cap.

"Listen you!" snarled Gil. He crouched a little and his eyes widened, unblinkingly, like a basilisk.

Powers walked in between Gil and the others. "Sit down," he said coldly. "Keep your hands away from those six-guns. I'm the big auger

150

here. You willing to listen? To take commands? To stop feudin' with the others?"

Gil bristled a little and for a moment it seemed as though he'd even attack his own brother, and then he underwent a change. He smiled. "Sure, Powers," he said easily.

Powers turned. "That goes for the rest of you. The woman is gone. She was only a *puta* anyway. She can't talk now."

Gil felt for the makings. "She did a *little* talking. To me, anyway . . ." He began to fashion a cigarette, and for a split second his eyes flicked toward Buck Terrell. "Go on with the plan, Powers."

Buck leaned against the wall and began to form a quirly, his mind darting back into the past like a terrier seeking rats, trying to remember what had happened that morning of blood at Tres Jacales. Theresa had been in the other room when Fred Carpenter had rushed the front room in true Ranger style. In a matter of less than a few minutes Buck had tripped Carpenter, and the Ranger had knocked Gil over as he fell. Buck had stepped in to buffalo Gil, then had explained to Carpenter who he, Buck, was. Was it possible that Theresa had seen what Buck had done, and overheard the

151

conversation between Buck and Carpenter? Had she remembered when she sobered up that Buck had knocked her out? Maybe she had been conscious when Buck had dragged the dead stranger into the house and set the building afire. Maybe she had seen him plant the man's wallet and hat in the gully. Perhaps she had examined the body of the man Gil had shot down in the street and had known he was dead. Any of those questions in his mind might reveal his secret to Gil Rorkin. It would be like Gil to keep Buck dangling on a string, playing with him like a cat plays with a mouse, before he moved in for the cruel kill. Gil had told Powers back in Tres Jacales that he had not been sure the Ranger had buffaloed him. A Ranger had certainly buffaloed him, but it had been Buck Terrell, *not* Fred Carpenter. The booze had dulled his senses and his memory, but it was possible that some facts had returned to him after he had sobered up, and if Theresa had let slip any information at all, it would have added to Gil's suspicions.

Then another thought came to Buck. Something Powers Rorkin had said as he and Buck had ridden after Gil and Theresa as they left

Tres Jacales. "*It'll take a little more time with her*," he had said.

"What about the rest of the boys in the *corrida?*" asked Moss Beckett.

"I've paid them off," said Rorkin. "We don't need them anymore. I think this group here can handle anything that comes up. Besides, it's a larger share for each of us this way."

Tod Logan glanced at Cap Anthony who was still fiddling with the deck of cards. There was no expression on the lean man's face.

"We hit the train on the 23rd," said Rorkin. "Three days from now. That will give us time to set up relays of horses from the cavvy we have here. One man from each pair of you will take spare horses to a designated place say twenty miles from the railroad. When we pull leather from the raid, we can drive the first horses to death if we have to, then pick up the spares and keep going. We can cache food and water with the relay horses. You men can decide which of you will take out the spare horse. Might not be a bad idea to take two spares for each man, ride the second of your horses until it drops, leading the third mount. By that time we ought to be well away from the railroad, scattered in different directions."

Blas Perez nodded his head. "*Bueno*," he said. He pared a fingernail with the edge of his knife. "I will take out the horses for us, Moss."

Cap Anthony placed the deck of cards on the table. "I'll do the same for us, Tod," he said.

Buck thought quickly. There was no chance he could thwart the raid on the payroll train singlehandedly. He had to get word out to Captain Dan Lynch of the Frontier Battalion. "I'll take out the spares for us, Boss," he said.

Rorkin shook his head. "Let Gil do it," he said.

Gil opened his mouth to protest, and then he shut it, glancing secretively at Buck. He began to form a cigarette with his long, capable hands. Once again the chilly feeling crept over Buck's flesh. *How much did Gil Rorkin know?*

The remainder of the meeting was taken up by details, much of which passed by Buck entirely. Somehow he had to get word out to Lynch. Someone he could trust must contact Lynch. Then the thought of India Reeves came to him. He'd have to take a chance on her, but the problem would be to leave the Rorkin rancho and get to her. It would have been a cinch if he had been detailed by Powers Rorkin to take out the spare horses.

There would be much to do within the next few days. The men with the horses would leave some hours before dawn so as to be well on the way before daylight. There would be just time enough for them to plant the horses and then rendezvous near the railroad for the raid. There would also be much for those left at the rancho to do and none of them could leave until it was time for the raid. Buck had to get out of there that very night, contact India and talk her into contacting Lynch.

The meeting broke up at ten o'clock. Buck walked slowly to his quarters and kicked the door shut. He dropped onto his bunk, lit a cigarette and stared up at the dim ceiling.

An hour passed by and the rancho was as quiet as the grave. Buck took off his boots and slung them around his neck. He checked his Colt and derringer, then eased up the back window of the room to peer out into the thick darkness. The windmill was softly humming in the night breeze. The trees swayed gently back and forth. Buck stepped outside and flattened himself against the wall. He peered towards the corrals. He didn't want to take a chance on disturbing the horses this time of night and those damnable dogs might get wind of him.

There was no sign of the vicious brutes. He walked silently across the hard-packed ground and slipped into the shadows of the small motte near the banked-earth water tank. He turned and looked back toward the main building. It was as black as the ace of spades. Rorkin had paid off the extra men so there was nothing to fear from them.

Buck walked toward the fence beyond the water tank. He turned to look back again and froze in his tracks as he heard a low growl. One of the dogs had scented him. Slowly, ever so slowly, Buck worked off his jacket and bound it about his left arm and then he drew out his knife and opened the big blade. He backed toward the fence, hoping he could get over it before the dog launched his attack. The dog moved forward slowly, its nails clicking on the hard packed earth. The growl came again.

Buck glanced toward the fence. "Take it easy," he said to the dog.

The dog hesitated at the familiar voice. It was then that Buck recognized the only female of the four dogs, the bitch named Liz, and she was the worst of the bunch. Liz tilted her head to one side and growled again and then she launched herself at Buck, jaws wide open for a ripping slash at him. He thrust forward his left arm, ramming the protected forearm between the jaws, while he brought up a knee into her belly and thrust hard for her throat with the keen blade. He missed the target and Liz hit the ground, trying to free her jaws from the entangling cloth while her hind legs raked savagely at Buck's shins. Teeth bored into the jacket and met flesh in penetrating pain.

Buck dropped his right knee hard on her taut throat, forcing the protected arm further and further between the gaping jaws while she struggled frenziedly. Once again teeth bored into flesh. Buck winced and cursed as he felt the blood run down his arm. Sweat ran down his sides. The struggling dog squirmed out from beneath his knee and he struck savagely, again and again, plunging the honed steel into her belly and throat. Blood splattered against his face, half blinding him. She growled and tried to break free but he raked the blade across her throat from ear to ear. She struggled convulsively and then lay still, staining the ground with her life's blood.

Sick as he was there was no time to waste. He dragged her to the fence, then went back and scuffed dirt over the blood stains while holding his left arm up to keep his blood from dripping from his fingers. He climbed the fence and dragged her through the wire. She was damnably heavy but he had no choice. He found a shallow gully and dropped her into it, covering her with a mat of dry brush and loose rock, hoping to God the other dogs wouldn't smell her out.

He staggered a little as he walked. The aftermath of the fierce, insensate battle with the powerful bitch dog had drained much of his strength from him. It was almost worse than having to fight a man. He broke into a slow trot until he reached the fence and then went into a low shed that stood there. He closed the door and peeled back his left shirt sleeve. He lit a match and examined the wounds. They were more painful than dangerous. He bound his arm with his bandanna and then wiped the blood from his hands and face with straw. He needed a drink but knew he had no time to waste looking for liquor that night.

He took an old halter from a nail hook and crawled out of a back window into the wide field and looked back toward the other buildings. There was no sight nor sound of anyone as yet. He walked quickly across the field, feeling the blood running down his shins where the bitch had raked him. There were horses at the far side of the field and he hoped that none of them would set up a racket. He stopped and watched them. They were restless at his presence. He walked slowly toward them and whistled softly. One of them detached itself from the cavvy and galloped toward him and then stopped. He looked toward the buildings. They were still dark and quiet. He whistled again. The horse came a little closer. Buck recognized her as a friendly little mare. He walked softly toward her and she came to meet him, whinnying softly in pleasure. She shied and blew when she caught the scent of blood but by that time he had twisted a powerful hand into her mane and had clamped her mouth shut with the other hand, talking quietly into her ear as he did so. She quietened down and he put the halter on her and led her to a gateway. He opened it and led her through and then closed the gate behind him. A few moments later he was on the road.

The wind had begun to shift by this time and as it did so it carried something ominous with it; something Buck could hear above the steady drumming of the mare's hooves on the hard road; the mournful baying of dogs from the Rorkin rancho was brought to him on the night wind.

9

THE Reeves rancho was a dark cluster of buildings below the mule ear peaks. Not a light showed. Buck had heard that the rancho was hardly a paying proposition. A few cattle and a few hands to take care of them. Tod Logan had said that all India Reeves needed was a good man to breed her and take care of the rancho, meaning himself of course. India Reeves was a right smart filly, and pretty to boot, and getting beyond the age when most girls in that isolated country had married. Women were at a premium in the Big Bend.

Buck tethered the mare to a tree and padded down the long dark slope toward the fence that surrounded the buildings. The barking of a dog did not greet him, unusual for a rancho not to have a dog, but, in any case, Buck Terrell had had quite enough of dogs for some time to come.

He worked his way between the fence strands and walked softly toward the dark house. The wind moaned uneasily around the mule ear peaks. There was a feel of tension in the cool night air. Buck didn't have too much time to spend here. He had to get back to the Rorkin place before he was missed. If they found out he had left the rancho he'd never be able to explain why he had left. He'd likely never be able to explain anything else in his mortal life.

He stepped up on the wide porch and tried the front door. It opened easily to the touch. He padded into the dark living room and down a hallway that led to the rear of the house, pausing at each door to listen. Two of the rooms were as silent as the grave, in the third room the sound of dry snoring suggested the presence of a man. He hoped that India Reeves didn't snore like that. The end room gave results. He eased open the door and was instantly aware of the feminine aura of the room. Buck took his courage into his hands and stepped into the room.

"That's far enough," she said from the darkness. The crisp double clicking of a gun hammer sounded loudly in the quietness.

"It's Spade Cleburne," he said.

"It didn't take you long to find your way back here, *Mister* Cleburne," she said. "Raise your hands."

He raised his hands. "Look, Miss India," he said quickly. "I did you a favor by bringing your uncle back here. I haven't got much time."

"For what?" she said dryly.

He took a step closer.

"Stay where you are," she snapped. "I'm quite a good shot, Mister Cleburne."

"You said once that there was something different about me," he said. "You were curious about me. I can satisfy that curiosity, if you'll give me a chance."

"Go on," she said.

He had to make his play now, win or lose. He couldn't handle the deadly game alone much longer. There was no one else in that country he could trust. "I want you to get a message to Captain Dan Lynch of the Frontier Battalion, Texas Rangers, at Ysleta."

"Why?" she demanded.

"*I'm* a Texas Ranger, Miss India. My real name is Buck Terrell. I've been working under-cover in the Rorkin *corrida* to try to find the men who have murdered four Rangers in this country."

She moved a little and he saw her silhouette against the window. She was clad in a flowing

163

nightgown, with her bare shoulders soft in the dimness. Something else shone dully in the faint light from the window—the blued metal of a gun barrel.

"Why do you tell me this now?" she said.

"I need help."

"So? Why did you come to me?"

"Powers Rorkin plans to raid the payroll train for the Lone Hills Mines on the 23rd, three days from now. The train slows down at Estacado, then moves upgrade at a slow rate until it reaches the end of Tornillo Canyon. Rorkin plans to have his men drop atop the cars, stop the engine, then blow a way into the payroll car. After the raid, the *corrida* splits up, some of them heading north, others west, and others south, after caching the payroll. Fresh horses will be hidden on each of the three escape routes so that the *corrida* can make all possible speed in escaping. If Captain Lynch is notified by telegraph within the next twelve hours, he'll have enough time to trap the outlaws. Where is the closest telegraph station?"

"At Herter Junction," she said.

"How far away is that?"

"Almost fifty miles."

Buck whistled softly. "It will take some riding," he said.

"I can do it," she said quietly.

"Will you?" He searched her face with questioning eyes.

She laughed softly. "It's quite a story, Mister Cleburne."

"Terrell," he corrected.

"*Whoever* you are," she said.

"Can I put down my hands?" he asked.

"Why?"

"I'll prove that I am a Ranger."

"Go on," she said. "Just don't make any unusual movements."

He lowered his hands and pulled off his left boot. Pinned inside the lining was his Ranger star, five-pointed, set inside a circle. He held it out to her, snapping a match on his thumbnail as he did so. Her eyes were fixed on his face.

She eyed the star. "They say the Rorkin *corrida* have killed four Texas Rangers. Might not that be one of their stars?"

"It might," he admitted, "but it isn't."

"I don't know whether to believe you or not."

"Do you think I'd tell anyone of the raid on

the payroll train if I actually am one of the outlaws?"

"It doesn't make sense," she agreed. She lowered the pistol, and then placed it on a table. "Something told me the first time I saw you that you were no ordinary man. It wouldn't have been like one of Powers Rorkin's men to bring my uncle back here when he was drunk."

"You'll do it then?"

She hesitated. "Must you go back? Can't you take the message and come back with the Rangers?"

"You seem to forget why I am working under cover in the Rorkin *corrida*, Miss India," he said. "We have no clues as yet as to who murdered those four Rangers."

"Does it matter that much? If you prevent the raid and capture them, won't that serve the same purpose?" she asked.

"They are murderers, Miss India. They murdered four Rangers. No one has paid as yet for those murders. One of the four was my younger brother, and one of the others was my best friend."

There was no further argument from India Reeves. "I'll leave as quickly as I can," she said. "I won't know what to tell my uncle."

"You can't trust him with the truth?"

"If he is sober, yes, but if he starts drinking he'll never keep it quiet. I'll have to take him along I suppose."

He repeated the message to her and she memorized it. He turned his back as she dressed quickly. Time was passing at too great a rate to suit him. Any minute now one of the *corrida* might look for him in his room. The dead dog might be found. The mare might be missed. Buck Terrell's life was hanging by the most tenuous of threads.

"You can turn around now," she said. She was close to him. "Please don't go back to that awful place."

Buck turned and found that she was close to him, that she was almost touching him. For a moment he looked down into her oval face, dimly seen in the darkness, and then, as though they were drawn together by some deep emotional magnet, they were pressed against each other, body and lips, and Buck Terrell, who had lost a fragment of himself the first time he had said goodbye to India Reeves, knew that he had found it again. He had completely lost his heart to her.

There was little time to lose. They must part

now, perhaps never to see each other again. A last, clinging kiss, and then Buck left the darkened house. She'd have to make some excuse to her uncle, and the presence of Buck Terrell would hardly make an excuse sound plausible. Buck walked softly across to the fence, and he did not see the pale, taut face of Carl Justin peering at him from an open window.

Buck passed between the strands of fence wire and rode the mare back through the darkness toward the Rorkin rancho. Everything depended now on India Reeves. If she failed, Buck would be alone, facing as tough a *corrida* as he had ever seen, each man a skilled professional in his own right; each man a killer.

He reached the fence pasture where he had found the mare. It was several hours before dawn. The rancho seemed asleep. He turned the lathered mare loose and slapped her on the rump. She trotted away in the darkness. Buck walked rapidly toward the far end of the field, passing the place where he had buried the dead dog. It was undisturbed. He crawled through the fence and padded along the side of the big water tank and stopped at the end closest to the corrals and the rancho buildings, testing the darkness with his senses, his Colt cocked and ready in his hand. There was no sound of the other three dogs. He was puzzled. He was downwind of them but even so they should have been alerted by now.

He rounded the tank and bent over, taking advantage of every scrap of cover as he worked his way back toward his quarters. He paused in the little motte and scanned the buildings. He shrugged. It was too quiet and peaceful to suit him, but maybe his luck was holding. He started across the open ground. Halfway across to the quarters, in the open, with not a shred of cover, he heard voices from the far end of the biggest of the buildings. A dog barked. His heart skipped a beat and his blood seemed to congeal. He darted across to the rear wall of his quarters and flattened himself against the wall as three men walked toward the corrals with a dog leaping and barking about their striding legs. It must be Blas Perez, Cap Anthony and Gil Rorkin, getting the horses to take out to the designated hiding places.

Another dog appeared near the corrals. He cocked his head toward the three outlaws, then looked steadily at the place where Buck Terrell stood flattened against the wall. Buck had no choice. He worked his way sideways, thrust a leg into his room, looked back and saw the dog racing toward his window, ears laid flat, tail straight as a ramrod and pure hell in his yellow eyes.

"Jesus God!" said Buck. He pushed the window down. It stuck several inches from the bottom. He stripped off his clothing and threw it on a chair. He skimmed his hat at a peg and saw it settle there. He dived for the bed and yanked the thin blanket up about him just as the dog thrust his nose under the window and growled like a demon straight from hell's own parlor.

"What's wrong, Hammerhead?" said Gil Rorkin from outside the room.

"Damned hound is sure interested in something," said Cap Anthony. "He usually don't miss much that goes on."

Hammerhead was growling up a storm.

"You in there, Cleburne?" said Cap Anthony.

"Yeh!" snapped Buck. "What the hell is going on?"

"Damned dog is all excited."

"Well, tell him to go get excited somewheres else," said Buck sleepily.

There was a short silence. Then Gil Rorkin spoke. "Were you up just a little while ago?"

"No," said Buck. "Why?"

"It ain't like Hammerhead to get excited about nothing."

"What the hell do you want me to do about it?" snapped Buck.

"Damn you, Cleburne! Don't you talk to me that way!"

"Come on, Gil," said Blas Perez. "Settle things with him later."

"Yeh," said Cap Anthony with a laugh. "After we get the loot from the train."

Their boots grated on the hard earth. Buck wiped the cold sweat from his forehead and rolled a cigarette. He lit it and drew in the comforting smoke. He could hear the three men talking at the corrals as they roped and saddled their horses. In a little while he heard the thudding of many hooves as they rode off into the darkness, leading the extra mounts. There was one thing he did not know. Gil Rorkin had been near the fence that bordered the large field in which the mare was running loose. She had galloped up to the corral for company and Gil had noticed her lathered coat, even though she had been rolling in the dust.

Blas Perez flicked his dark eyes to Gil. "She's been doing a lot of running, this *caballo*," he said.

"Yeh," said Gil. He looked thoughtfully back at the darkened buildings. After the three of them had passed the earthen water tank he glanced back at the buildings again. The mare was known to be lazy. It wasn't like her to gallop up a storm if she wasn't forced into it.

"Come on, Gil!" said Cap Anthony. "We ain't got all night!"

Buck Terrell was up at dawn, his thoughts with India Reeves as she rode north to Herter Junction. He had to stay with the Rorkin *corrida*. He couldn't run now, nor would he run, for the memories of the deaths of his brother Frank and that of Kelly Ledbetter were etched on his mind, as well as the deaths of the other two Rangers, Francisco Armenderiz and Cooke Durkee. There was sheer cold hate in his heart for these men with whom he now rode. He had heard enough talk from them to know they had been responsible for the deaths of the four Rangers. Justice would be served if the Rangers under Dan Lynch could thwart the raid on the payroll train and bring in the Rorkin *corrida* for that crime, as well as for questioning, but there was a quality in Buck Terrell that demanded much more from these killers. He wanted the personal satisfaction of facing them with the accusations, then either bringing them to justice, or making them pay for their bloody crimes under the smoking muzzles of his guns.

The cook had been discharged, so the men remaining at the rancho had to shift for themselves. Buck ate alone. It was his job to gather together the gear needed for the raid on the payroll train. Tools, rope, extra cartridges, camping gear and, last but not least, the can of Kepauno Giant blasting powder required for the operation. He had been sorely tempted to empty out the powder and substitute something else, but he had realized that perhaps Dan Lynch could not reach Tornillo Canyon in time. If the outlaws attempted to use the powder and it did not explode, they'd come looking for Buck Terrell with hell in their eyes.

One of the three remaining days passed with agonizing slowness, and on the morning of the second day, Powers Rorkin led his small party to the north. A loaded burro carried the extra gear and the blasting powder. The other three men of the *corrida* were to rendezvous at a

173

designated place near Tornillo Canyon, but Powers Rorkin had not mentioned the rendezvous place to his group, or, if he had, he had not mentioned it to Buck Terrell. Powers Rorkin was not one to divulge his plan in entirety to his men. Buck remembered something that India Reeves had said about Powers. *"He's just as mad as Gil, though in a different way. Powers Rorkin is on a one way road. To complete power or sudden death."*

They camped that night in a canyon some miles to the south of Tornillo Canyon. By this time, according to Buck's calculations, India Reeves would have sent her message to Captain Lynch, and Lynch, with his usual speed and efficiency, would have made his arrangements by now.

That night Buck lay for a long time in his blankets, staring up at the dark blue sky, stippled with its winking stars, listening to the night wind sighing softly through the great trough of the canyon. Somewhere, far to the south, came the melancholy crying of a coyote, to be followed by another sound, equally lonely in quality, the long drawn whistling of a locomotive as it passed somewhere to the north.

During the night Cap Anthony and Blas

Perez showed up, but there was no sign of Gil Rorkin. Hours before the faint pewter traces of dawn marked the eastern sky, the *corrida* arose and rode to silent, brooding Tornillo Canyon, a narrow-walled trough, thick in darkness, through which the cold wind moaned softly, swaying the thorny vegetation and rolling tumbleweeds along the narrow right of way far below.

Rorkin's low-spoken orders set the group to work, and as he worked along with the others, Buck began to realize that Powers Rorkin, in his field, was a certified specialist. While Cap stood guard on a naked ridge above the canyon, the others constructed a low barricade of pegged logs, dragged from a nearby bosque in a low spot near the canyon. Behind the logs they piled rock. The contraption was placed on a slope overlooking the narrowest part of the canyon, where the train had barely enough room to squeeze through on its way to the mines, some miles to the west. Lariats were fastened to the pegs and laid on the ground ready to pull the pegs loose at the time required.

Buck Terrell peered down into the canyon. When the logs fell away, the rocks would fall into the canyon, effectively blocking the locomotive. There were several places where a man could crouch, unseen, until the train was stopped, and then he would be able to drop easily to the roof of a car, or onto the tender.

It was hot and heavy work despite the coolness of the night and the searching wind. When the rock fall was completed, brush was cut and dragged to it, and the logs and rocks were covered so that it was almost impossible to see them.

Moss Beckett occupied himself in making fuses for his cans of blasting powder. Buck laid out the tools that might be required. Axes and pry bars might be needed to force their way into a blasted car.

Tod Logan wiped the sweat from his dusty face. "Trust Gil to be missing when this type of work has to be done," he growled to Buck.

Buck nodded. "Maybe he had farther to go," he said easily.

"Hell!" said Blas. "Only to Negra Canyon."

Buck tested the edge of an axe with his thumb. "Where's that?"

"Just this side of Herter Junction," said Tod.

Buck almost dropped the axe. "Maybe it's a rough trail," he suggested.

"No," said Blas. "There's only one trail

cutting through the mountains toward Herter Junction from this area. Coming or going, you have to use it, or go miles out of your way. Negra Canyon opens off that trail."

Cold sweat dewed Buck's face. He remembered too well what India Reeves had told him about her association with Gil Rorkin. "I can't stand Gil Rorkin," she had said. "Gil sickens me. When my father was alive he stayed away from the place. For a time he almost drove us from this country." Supposing, by a cruel trick of fate, that Gil ran into India Reeves, riding alone in the vicinity of Negra Canyon. It was a lonely, almost completely deserted country. If Gil had been drinking . . . Buck passed a hand across his face. Words spoken by another person who well knew Gil Rorkin came into Buck's mind. Blas Perez had neatly catalogued Gil. "The Kid likes his women as well as he does the sight and smell of blood. But, he never goes after the women unless he is very drunk."

Tod Logan rolled a cigarette and lit it. "Well, anyways, Gil can't get drunk in Negra Canyon unless he has a bottle with him."

Blas laughed softly. "Herter Junction is one quarter railroad station, one quarter general store and one half saloon. Not bad for having only four buildings there."

"Yeh," said Tod. "I forgot about that. That's all we need. Gil drunk as a coot shooting off his big mouth in one of them saloons."

Buck began to fashion a cigarette. It was the woman Theresa who had added to the sordid picture of Gil Rorkin. "I love him. No matter what he does to me I love him. He is very bad at times. There are bruises still on my body from the last time."

Tod blew a smoke ring. "Well, he's missed out on getting things ready for this deal."

Blas laughed again. "He'll show up in time for the blood-letting. He can smell blood like a shark."

There was little to do now but wait for daylight. To wait for daylight, thought Buck, *and* Gil Rorkin. The train was due to pass through Tornillo Canyon about dusk that day. The train crew would never spot the rock fall above them, not until it cascaded down atop them and blocked their progress. By then it would be too late. It would be too late unless Captain Dan Lynch and his men of the Frontier Battalion, Texas Rangers had been alerted and had had time to reach Tornillo Canyon. The tough *corrida* would have little trouble cracking open the payroll car. In a matter of perhaps no more than half an hour to forty-five minutes they'd be on their way from the scene of death and destruction with the big payroll, riding their horses to death if necessary, to the secret places where the fresh horses had been concealed. It was Indian-style tactics. When the *corrida* was well scattered and the loot well cached it would be almost impossible to round up the outlaws. If Captain Lynch and his Texas Rangers did not show up it would devolve upon one man, Buck Terrell, to thwart the raid, and the odds against this eventuality seemed to be mountain high and canyon deep to Buck himself.

"*Es de dia*," said Blas Perez. He waved a hand toward the east. The eastern sky was faintly, so very faintly tinged with gray. The wind was dying, shifting and wavering uncertainly back and forth.

Tod Logan did a jaw-breaking yawn. "Maybe a man can get in a little sleep by now. A man don't mind this kind of work but it sure plays hell with his sleep and his digestion."

Blas grinned. "But the pay is good, eh, *amigo?*"

"I got no argument there, Blas," admitted Tod.

They rode back into the concealing hills and watered their mounts at a little *tinaja* and then led the horses further into the concealment of the thick brush and stunted trees. There was nothing to do now but to sleep, or smoke and think, as they waited for the train. Everything was ready in exact detail, as planned. The train would announce its own coming as far east as Estacado as it slogged and puffed its way up the grade. There was plenty of time for the *corrida* to get into position. Everything was neatly wrapped up into a surprise package and the string would be pulled by Powers Rorkin when the time came. He had thought of everything.

10

THE shadows were lengthening over the open country to the east of Tornillo Canyon. A faint and fitful breeze had sprung up, whispering dryly through the canyon, rustling the brush and stunted trees. High over the canyon a hawk hung as though pasted against the blue of the sky. It was so very quiet and peaceful to outward appearances.

Powers Rorkin drained his coffee cup and got up from his squatting position to walk away from the waterhole, looking up to where Blas Perez lay hidden in a site where he could see Tornillo Canyon and also the country to the north.

Cap Anthony shifted his chew and spat copiously at a gecko lizard, splattering it with the juice. "Maybe I called the shot," he said. He looked at Powers. "The Boss is all right. But that damned brother of his . . . I'll bet he's belting the booze right now in some *cantina*. Oh sure, he'll show up, *after* we take the risks."

He spat again. "Over my dead body he'll get a cut of the loot."

Tod Logan grinned. "Maybe that's the way he figures it. Over your dead body."

Moss Beckett opened his eyes and rolled over to raise himself on an elbow. He looked toward Powers. "Maybe something happened to the Kid," he said quietly.

Cap Anthony laughed. "We should be so lucky," he said.

Buck Terrell rolled a cigarette. Time was moving apace. He had no knowledge that Captain Lynch was anywhere in the vicinity if he had been alerted by India Reeves. Dusk was on the way, bringing with it the payroll train. Where was Gil Rorkin? There was no choice now but for Buck to try to prevent the attack on the train. It would be like charging hell with a fire bucket—Ranger style.

"Listen!" said Moss Beckett.

Far across country, faintly heard, came the whistling of a locomotive. The sound died away in the hills.

"She's a good ways from Estacado yet," said Tod.

Maybe Gil had discovered that the Rangers were on the way to Tornillo Canyon. Maybe he

182

actually knew who Buck was. Buck stood up and rolled a fresh cigarette. He reached for his rifle.

"Where you going?" asked Moss Beckett.

"Thought I'd ride over to the canyon," said Buck easily.

"We've got plenty of time," said Moss. "Besides, we ride *together*, Cleburne."

Buck shrugged. "All the same to me," he said.

"Cleburne!" called out Powers.

Buck walked over to the man. "Yes, Boss?" he said.

"Get up that ridge and see if you can spot Gil." Rorkin looked back at the camp. "I don't want any more of that talk about Gil. He'll be here! He has to be here!"

"Sure, Boss," said Buck. He walked over to his horse and saddled it, thrusting his rifle into the scabbard. He rode up the ridge where Blas Perez was on lookout. The whistling of the locomotive came again. There was still plenty of time before it reached Estacado for the long, slow haul up Tornillo Canyon.

Buck glanced at Blas Perez. It wasn't dark enough for Buck to Indian up on the sharp-eyed Mex, and even if it was dark it wouldn't be easy to surprise Cuchillo. A wild thought had come to Buck that he might just be able to pick off the *corrida*, one by one, but the odds were against it. He looked to the east and saw a faint scarf of smoke rising beyond Estacado, which was nothing more than a cluster of shacks built for the track crews, and most of the time the place was empty of life except when work was being done on the tracks. There was no work being done on the tracks at this time. Powers Rorkin had checked into that.

Buck looked down toward the camp. The four outlaws had saddled up and were leading their horses toward the west end of the canyon. Buck could just make out the powder cans hanging from Moss Beckett's saddle. He looked toward the spot where they had built the rock fall. Two horses, one at either end, could easily drag the pegs out of the ground, thus releasing the massed rocks to fall into the canyon below. Even if Buck accounted for Blas Perez, there were still four of them to contend with, and the odds that Buck could master them would be insurmountable.

Buck uncased the field glasses all of Rorkin's men carried as part of their equipment. He adjusted the focus and swept the country to the north. A thread of dust was rising half a mile away, although the source of the dust was hidden from view.

Blas Perez called down to Buck. "You see the dust, *amigo?*"

"Yes. Maybe we'd better warn Rorkin."

"Why? It can only be a lone rider, perhaps two at the most."

"But who are they?" called Buck. Damn Blas Perez and his hawk's eyes! The dust might be stirred up by Dan Lynch's boys.

Perez raised his glasses. "It is all right," he said. "I see them now. They are still hidden from your view, Spade. Two riders." Perez laughed softly.

"What's so funny?" called out Buck.

"One of them is Gil Rorkin."

"Yes?"

"The other is a woman! Wait until Powers sees his baby brother bringing a woman into this deal. Hawww!"

The cold sweat of fear broke out on Buck Terrell. A woman! "Can you see who she is?" he called out. The view of them was still obstructed for Buck by the lay of the land.

There was a long pause. "By Chihuahua!" said Blas.

"Who is it?" snapped Buck.

"Why get excited? A woman is a woman." Perez laughed again. "It is the Reeves woman! The one whose nose is always in the air!"

"Jesus God," said Buck under his breath. Maybe she had betrayed him! Maybe her attitude toward him had been that of a skilled actress! If she had betrayed him, then she had not alerted the Rangers. If she had informed Gil, then Buck's life wasn't worth a plugged *centavo*. There was little time to lose. He could get away easily enough from Blas Perez, and the odds were that Powers Rorkin wouldn't bother chasing him, not with sixty thousand dollars being pulled toward the saddlebags of the *corrida* by the oncoming train.

Buck glanced toward his horse. It was a good one, a blocky dun who'd carry him fast and far. Buck took a step toward the dun. Far to the east the locomotive whistled again.

Perez lowered his glasses. "The Killer and his woman," he said in an amused voice.

Buck thrust his left foot into the stirrup and gripped the reins.

Perez leaned back against the rock behind him. "Just in time to help in the train attack," he said. "The Ranger Killer!"

Buck lowered his foot and dropped the reins. He looked up at Cuchillo. "What did you call him?" he asked.

"Ranger Killer. We used to call him that until Powers made us stop. Said it was too dangerous." Perez began to fashion a cigarette. "That damned fool thought it was quite a honor to be called Ranger Killer." He grinned.

"I can imagine," said Buck softly.

"You! Up there!" yelled Powers Rorkin from below them on the Tornillo Canyon side. "What's going on?"

"Gil is coming," said Perez.

"*Bueno!*"

"With a woman," yelled back Perez. His broad flat face was expressionless.

"With a woman . . . with a woman . . . with a woman . . ." echoed from the far side of Tornillo Canyon, and everyone of the *corrida* could plainly hear the echo.

Buck looked down at Powers Rorkin. Even in the gathering shadows and at that distance, Buck could see the taut, set look on the man's lean face.

"Send him down, Cuchillo," said Powers at last. "Spade, you come on down right now."

"The train has stopped at Estacado," called out Tod Logan.

That would give them a little more time. There was hardly a chance the plan would go wrong. Everything was ready. Everyone knew his part, for they had been drilled in their roles by Powers Rorkin. Nothing could go wrong . . . *nothing*.

Buck glanced toward the two approaching riders. He'd have to cast the dice now, odds or no. He mounted the dun and rode down toward the wide rock shelf that overlooked the narrow part of the canyon. He could see the rock fall from where he was. Moss Beckett was crouched further along the rock shelf, about where the cars would be halted, his fused powder cans close at hand. Cap Anthony and Tod Logan had fastened the lariats from the pegs to their saddlehorns, ready at a word from Powers Rorkin to lash the horses along the shelf and release the rock fall.

Buck dismounted beside Rorkin. The leader looked down into the canyon. "You'll come with me," he said. "Tod and Cap will take care of the engine crew. We'll cover Moss while he sets his charges."

"What about Gil?" asked Buck casually.

Powers' face darkened. "Let the damned fool sit and watch us," he snarled.

Buck rolled a cigarette and handed it to Powers. "Take it easy, Boss," he said. "It's the Reeves woman with him."

Rorkin's face whitened beneath the tan. "By God!" he said. "I thought he'd have some tramp with him."

"Hardly able to get rid of a woman like India Reeves without a big stink blowing up, eh, Boss?" said Buck. He lit Rorkin's cigarette.

Rorkin shook his head. "The Kid always had a soft spot in his head for her. Seems like when he first met her she liked him too. After that, well, it doesn't take the Kid long to start making advances. He picked the wrong filly with India Reeves." He looked up the slope. "Beats the hell out of me what he's up to this time."

"Train starting up again," called Tod Logan.

"She'll reach here in twenty minutes," said Rorkin.

Hooves clattered on the slopes beyond the canyon. Buck looked toward Gil Rorkin and at the girl who rode beside him. Her great eyes picked out Buck. Gil slid from the saddle. He walked toward Buck and Powers. Buck wet his dry lips. The Kid was too fast for Buck but Buck would have to draw, shoot and kill the instant Gil revealed that Buck had been betrayed.

"What the hell do you mean by bringing that woman here?" snapped Powers Rorkin.

"Wait a minute," said Gil. "I ran into her at Herter Junction."

"You had no business being there," said his brother.

"Forget about that," said Gil quickly. "She had that drunken uncle of hers with her. Carl Justin. I didn't know she was in town. Justin was getting drunk. He shot off his mouth."

"So?"

Gil paused. He glanced at Buck and then back at India.

"Go on!" said Powers.

Gil turned and hooked a thumb over his gun belt, his hand inches above the butt of his right-hand Colt. "She was dictating a message to the telegraph operator at Herter Junction. A message to Captain Dan Lynch of the Frontier Battalion, Texas Rangers, warning him that the Rorkin *corrida* was going to hit the payroll train here at Tornillo Canyon on the twenty-third."

"For the love of God," said Powers Rorkin. "How did she find out about the raid?"

"*Quien sabe?*" said Gil quietly. "Anyway, she didn't send the message. I put the fear of God into the telegrapher, and slipped him a hundred bucks besides, to keep his mouth shut."

"How do you know he kept the deal?" demanded Powers.

Gil grinned. "Wait a minute," he said.

"What about Justin? Maybe he warned Lynch!"

Gil shook his head. "Carl Justin won't ever shoot off his mouth again. As for the message being sent, I cut the wires between Herter Junction and El Paso half a dozen times while I was chasing this filly."

Powers nodded. "You're using your head," he said. "Anyone see you take care of Carl Justin?"

"Only her," said Gil.

Powers' hard eyes flicked toward the girl. "What do you plan to do with her now?" he asked.

Gil shrugged. "I didn't want to get rid of her. You always said it wasn't wise to fool around with a respectable woman. You said a man can

191

get into trouble quicker that way than any other way."

"The Kid is learning," grunted Tod Logan.

Buck looked at India and for the first time he noticed the dark bruises on her lovely face, and the fact that her slim wrists were bound together and tied to the saddlehorn. She hadn't talked or Buck Terrell would have been dead at her feet by now.

"We haven't time to fool with her now," said Powers. "Take her out of sight, Gil. We'll hit the train, then take her with us." He laughed. "Maybe some of the payroll money will shut her pretty mouth. If it doesn't, there are other ways. . . ."

"Train's entering the east end of the canyon," called out Tod Logan.

Buck watched Gil help the girl from the saddle, making free with his hands as he did so, and Buck wondered what he had done to her while she had been bound helplessly. For one instant, blood seemed to redden his view of the two of them, and then he let cold, hard reason regain control. There was nothing he could do now. "Ranger Killer" Blas Perez had called the Kid. That name would brand the Kid with the death mark.

There was nothing to do now but wait. Buck could hardly prevent the train from being robbed. He'd take his chances of course if they were presented, but it was hardly likely. The chuffing of the oncoming Standard filled the canyon with noise. Smoke drifted up high as the engine fought to haul the cars along toward their destination with the Powers' *corrida*.

Then, quicker than Buck had expected, the Standard was in the narrow cut, approaching the place where the rocks were poised above it. Powers Rorkin held up a hand. He dropped it suddenly. Locomotive smoke swirled up from the deep cut as Tod Logan and Cap Anthony lashed their horses, freeing the heavy pegs from the ground. The logs slid a little, impelled by the great weight behind them, then they slid with a harsh grating sound over the brink, followed by the roaring flood of rocks, dirt and thick rising dust. The brakes of the Standard screeched like souls in torment as the fall struck the tracks ahead of it, completely blocking the way. The train had little speed on it so the locomotive, braked and held back by the weight of the tender and cars, nosed into the rock fall and stopped with a great swirling of smoke and steam rising above it in the dusk air.

"Now!" snapped Powers.

Tod and Cap slid from the edge of the rock ledge and landed lightly atop the piled coal in the tender, six guns in their hands, bandannas about their faces, hats pulled low. They started toward the open cab of the engine.

Powers Rorkin, followed by Gil, dropped atop the first car behind the tender. "Come on, Spade!" roared Powers.

Buck slid from the edge of the rocks. There was nothing else he could do. He landed heavily atop the baggage car and started running after the two masked Rorkin brothers. Moss Beckett had dropped atop the second car. Behind it was a flat car loaded with mining machinery and behind that was the rinky-dink, four-wheeled crummy. A man's head poked out of the window atop the crummy. Gil fired from the hip. Blood flooded the man's face and he fell back inside the caboose.

"Take it easy!" yelled Powers. "I don't want any more killing than we have to do!"

Buck pulled his bandanna up about his face. Rorkin knew the payroll was in the second car, although where and how he got his information was beyond Buck, and any of the others for that matter. Rorkin kept his informants to himself.

Buck looked back along the top of the cars. Tod Logan was running heavily after him. This was evidence that he and Cap had gotten the drop on the locomotive crew, and that Cap was holding them at gunpoint. Gil Rorkin passed along the top of the second car, climbed down to the flat car and ran back toward the caboose.

Tod climbed down the side of the second car and dropped to the side of the tracks. He pulled out his Colt and fired warning shots into the wooden side of the car.

Powers Rorkin stopped beside Moss. Moss was slamming a double-bitted axe into the top of the car. Splinters flew through the air. A gun shot sounded from the caboose and smoke swirled out of the windows. The Kid was killing again.

Buck picked up an axe and hefted it. Two good strokes and he could get rid of Moss and Powers. He looked down and saw Tod Logan looking up at him. "No one in this car!" called out Logan. He climbed up beside Buck and stood beside him.

Moss placed the first of his powder cans in the hole he had dug into the roof top. A gun sounded from inside the car. Moss grinned. "Trying to get me through the roof," he said.

He lit a cigar and jerked his head. "Dig two more holes. One in the middle, the other at the forward end. Pronto!"

There was nothing else Buck could do. He dug the middle hole while Tod hewed out the one at the end. Gil Rorkin climbed atop the caboose. "All clear back here!" he yelled.

Buck looked up. Blas Perez was on lookout up on the ridge. No one could approach the train without him spotting them and giving plenty of warning.

Moss Beckett planted two more of his charges and looked at Powers. Rorkin raised a hand for silence. He got down on his knees and yelled down into one of the chopped holes. "You men down there! I'll give you three minutes to open those doors or we'll blow you to hell!"

A gun shot sounded below. Rorkin cursed as he jumped to his feet and clapped a hand to his bleeding face.

"You hit, Boss?" asked Beckett.

"Only a splinter," said Rorkin. He looked at his waiting men. "Light the fuses, Moss."

Beckett walked from one end of the car to the other, lighting each fuse with his cigar in turn, each of them calculated nicely to burn at

196

the same interval and to explode at the same time.

"*Vamonos!*" said Powers Rorkin curtly. He climbed down the side of the car followed by Tod Logan. Buck went down a ladder on the other side and saw Gil standing on the same side of the train. Moss came down in a hurry. "Run!" he snapped. He ran toward the rear of the train.

There was nothing Buck could do. He legged it after the tall man followed by the sound of the sputtering fuses. It was getting darker and the canyon was filling with thick shadows.

The first charge blew with a shattering roar, followed almost instantaneously by the other two charges. Buck looked back. The car roof seemed to be rising impelled by invisible levitation. Then it fell sideways in a billowing of rank smoke while a tower of the smoke rose in the quiet air. The roaring of the explosion slammed back and forth between the walls of the canyon. It could be heard for miles.

Great splinters of shattered yellow wood sailed through the air like javelins to clatter against the rock sides of the deep cut. A man screamed insanely through the wreathing smoke. Then it was quiet again as the echoes died down the canyon. The smoke thickened and began to drift in the natural draft of the cut. Through the dimness the outlaws ran like ghouls toward the shattered car. A headless body lay beside the car, flooding the right-of-way with a red pool from the gaping hole where the neck had been. An arm lay against the track.

Powers Rorkin was first into the smoke filled interior of the car, pistol in hand. He looked back at his men with a cold smile on his face. "No resistance here," he said.

Buck climbed into the car. Great gouts of blood had splattered the walls and floor of the car. The interior was a shambles. Rorkin walked to the heavy safe, bolted to the floor of the car. "All right, Moss," he called.

Moss studied the safe, oblivious of the faceless corpse that lay to one side of it. He felt inside his shirt and pulled out a smaller charge which he fastened to one side of the safe door. "Get down at the far end of the car behind that stuff there," he said over his shoulder.

They took cover. The fuse hissed. The charge blew. The safe door banged open. Powers Rorkin ran to the safe and felt inside. "Chihuahua!" he said. "It's all here!" He pulled out packets of bills, neatly wrapped and bound with elastics. Buck, Moss and Tod gathered up the paper wealth. They carried it outside. Gil Rorkin brought up the burro. The money was dumped unceremoniously into the Kyacks on each side of the beast.

"Where's Cap?" said Gil.

"At the locomotive," said Tod.

A gun shot sounded, and then another. A man yelled. Metal clanged and another gun shot echoed against the narrow walls.

Moss and Gil ran toward the locomotive. Cap fell heavily from the engine and sprawled alongside the rail. Buck led the burro after Powers Rorkin.

"Damned if he didn't get both of them," said Moss Beckett. He looked down from the cab. "Neat as sin."

Gil rolled Cap's body over. A great bloody slash showed on the thin face. "They got him too. Must'a been with a coal scoop."

Powers Rorkin wet his thin lips. "No time to lose," he said. "You know what to do, Gil."

Gil drew a Colt and rapped out six slugs, full into the face of Cap Anthony, splattering blood, flesh and bone to all sides. Gil grinned. "Even his own momma wouldn't know that ugly face now," he said.

Buck looked quickly away, feeling for his makings. The green bile had risen in his throat and for a moment he was almost sure he was going to get sick, all over the right-of-way.

"*Vamonos!*" commanded Powers Rorkin.

They left the cut at the west end by clambering over the rock fall, with the burro climbing easily behind them as Powers led him on. In a matter of ten minutes they had all gathered together without a word being spoken amongst them, but there was no need for conversation. The looks on their tanned faces was enough to show how they felt. The job had been carried off exactly as planned and sixty thousand dollars had plunked easily into the till of the Rorkin *corrida*.

Behind them in the thickening dust the smoke hung in thick rifted layers over the deep railroad cut and slowly began to rise to stain the clear sky. The wind shifted it back and forth as though it was doing a voluptuous and sensuous dance of death for those who lay hidden below the mingled pall of smoke and dust. The train crew and the payroll guards kept mute company with the faceless corpse of Cap Anthony.

The hooves thudded on the hard ground. Now and then Buck glanced surreptitiously back toward the railroad cut of sudden death. He looked at the burro, trotting along, laden with ill-gotten wealth. Lastly he looked at the slim back of India Reeves as she rode beside her captor, Gil Rorkin. The odds against Buck were worse than they had ever been. A cold feeling settled within him. There was now more than just his own life at stake; there was, as well, the life of the young woman with whom he had fallen in love.

Buck took out his dollar watch as the *corrida* topped a ridge. Powers Rorkin had called the shot some days ago when he had said: "The whole job shouldn't take more than half an hour to forty-five minutes." Exactly forty-five minutes had passed since Powers Rorkin had dropped his hand to signal Cap Anthony and Tod Logan to release the rock fall.

Powers Rorkin led the way down the far side of the ridge, with the money-laden burro trotting briskly along behind him. Behind him came Gil, leading the horse upon which India Reeves rode captive. No one spoke. Five miles from the railroad line the trail threaded through a pass. Rorkin drew rein at the narrow mouth of the pass. "Logan and Perez," he said. "Stay here and watch for pursuit. Give us an hour's lead."

"What the hell!" snapped Tod Logan.

Powers lit a cigar. He looked at Logan over the flare of the match. "You questioning my orders?" he quietly asked. He looked sideways at Blas Perez and saw the same look upon the Mexican's face that was etched upon Tod Logan's face. "What's bothering you, Blas?" he added.

Blas smiled deprecatingly. "Well," he said slowly. "It is quite a lead, you must admit, *patron*."

Powers shifted in his saddle. "You think I'm planning to pull out on both of you and keep going with the loot, is that it?"

Blas seemed horrified. "God forbid that I should think of such a thing, *patron!*"

Rorkin nodded. "Gil," he said over his shoulder. "Hand that woman over to Moss. Stay here with Tod."

Gil turned quickly. "Jesus Christ!" he said. "Why *me?*"

"Why not?" asked Powers. "You're still one of the *corrida*, aren't you?"

"But you're my own brother!" cried Gil

202

angrily. His face flushed and his eyes were wide in his head.

"All the more reason you should stay," said Powers. His meaning was plain enough.

Buck Terrell began to fashion a quirly, watching this play between brother and brother. He saw fully now the capabilities of Powers Rorkin as a planner and leader. Gil hated to do what he was told to do. God, how he hated to obey! For a moment he sat there staring at his implacable older brother and then he flung the lead rope to Moss Beckett. Powers nodded. *Adelante!* he snapped. He touched the steel to his rangy gray and started for the mouth of the pass, followed by Moss and the girl, Blas Perez and Buck Terrell. Buck could not resist a sideways look at the face of Gil Rorkin and it seemed as though Gil was looking out of a smoky window of hell with the set face of a demon who knew nothing but hatred.

Rorkin hammered on through the echoing pass, never looking behind him. In an hour they were through the pass and descending the long slopes out onto the more level country with the mountain range through which they had passed forming an effective barrier to immediate pursuit, aided and abetted by the two hard-eyed riflemen Rorkin had left behind to hold the pass if there were immediate pursuit.

They had crossed the wide expanse of flats toward a range of broken hills, shimmering in the powerful heat of the day, when Rorkin paused and uncased his field glasses. He turned in his saddle and looked back toward the faint line that marked the mouth of the pass. "Dust," he said. "The boys are through the pass. Evidently there wasn't any pursuit." He cased the glasses and turned to ride along the base of the hills, avoiding the faint trace of road that led through the hills the easy way.

"The road is there, *patron*," said Blas, pointing toward the faint trace.

"Sure it is," said Powers, "and that's just what would be expected of us. We're riding *around* the hills."

"We'll need water, Boss," said Moss Beckett.

Rorkin did not answer. "Cuchillo," he said. "Stay here and direct the others. We ride seven miles west, then trend southwest. I'll have a man waiting there for you to show you the way."

Blas nodded. He reined in his sorrel and hooked a leg over his pie-plate pommel to shape a cigarette. His dark, enigmatic eyes watched the little party riding away from him. As long as he was with Gil Rorkin, he knew Powers Rorkin would never try to get away with all that loot.

Buck Terrell was waiting for the trio of dusty horsemen when they reached the point that had been designated by Powers Rorkin. He was squatting beside his dun when they came up, with a cigarette hanging from the corner of his mouth. The dusk was creeping across the hills and painting thick shadows in the draws. There was no sign of pursuit across the wide flats; no trace of dust or movement. Buck silently mounted and led them on through a hardly discernible notch in the hills. The moon was up when they entered a long shallow valley. Its light picked out the faded white canvas tilt of a two-wheeled *carreta* about which the advance group was waiting for the trio of horsemen.

Buck slid from his saddle. The tired horses were being watered from a spigoted barrel that protruded over the tailgate of the cart. The mingled odors of bacon, beans and coffee rose in the quiet air. A strange Mexican squatted beside the fire, ladling food into plates for Gil, Tod and Buck.

Powers Rorkin was seated on a rock, smoking

a cigar. "Eat up," he said. "We move out in twenty minutes."

"Our horses are beat," said Tod shortly.

Rorkin jerked a thumb behind him. "Look in that draw," he said quietly. A little cavvy of horses could be seen. "They're fresh," he said. "We'll use them tonight and take the others with us. We'll hole up at dawn, sleep all day, then go on again at dusk. Now eat!"

Blas rubbed his dusty face. "*Madre de Dios!*" he said. "The *patron* thinks of everything!"

Gil swiftly ladled the hot food into his mouth but his bitter eyes were upon his older brother. "Yeh," he said between mouthfuls.

Moss was filling the canteens. As each horse was watered he was led away by the strange Mexican and the saddle and gear were shifted to a fresh horse. Powers Rorkin was taking food sacks from the *carreta*. In twenty minutes all the saddles had been exchanged and the saddle-bags stuffed with food supplies, while Moss hung the full canteens from the saddles. The cart was now empty.

"Time's up!" said Powers as he lit a fresh cigar. "Kick out that fire, Buck!"

Buck kicked dirt over the dying embers. He

glanced sideways at the expressionless face of the outlaw leader. The devil had thought of everything just as Blas Perez had already commented.

"Mount up!" snapped Powers, like the commanding officer of a troop of veteran yellowlegs rather than the leader of a small *corrida* of outlaws.

The Mexican came to Powers as the man mounted his horse. He held out his hand. Powers dropped some goldpieces into it. "Keep the *boca* shut, eh, Santiago?" he said with a smile.

"Of course! Of course, Señor Rorkin!" said the Mexican. He hesitantly hefted the goldpieces. "There is, perhaps, a little more?"

"That's the agreed upon price, *amigo*," said Rorkin.

"That is so," said Santiago. "But one must have the insurance that the *boca* is more tightly closed."

Powers dropped two more goldpieces into the Mexican's hand. "*Adios*, Santiago," he said.

The Mexican trotted happily toward his empty *carreta* and his pair of dusty mules.

"He might still talk, *patron*," said Blas nervously.

207

Powers shifted his cigar from one side of his mouth to the other. He eased his Winchester .44/40 from its scabbard and as Santiago got up onto the seat of the cart, Rorkin swiftly raised the rifle and fired once. The heavy slug caught Santiago in the middle of the back and he fell to the ground, scattering the goldpieces about him. Rorkin ejected the empty brass hull. It tinkled on the hard-packed ground. "Get the gold, Blas," he said. "Cut loose those mules and add them to the cavvy."

"What if the cart and body are found?" asked Moss.

Powers smiled coldly around his cigar. "We'll be long gone by then," he said. "Besides, who's to know *we* did it?" He touched his horse with his spurs and rode down the shallow valley in the clear moonlight.

"He's a genius," said Blas Perez.

"Crap," said Gil Rorkin as he mounted his fresh horse with a full belly and a long drink of fresh water within him. "*I* could have thought of all this!"

No one spoke, but they all exchanged glances. They rode from the shallow valley with Tod and Buck driving the extra horses and the pair of mules, while Blas led on the burro and his Kyacks full of money. In a little while the valley was empty except for the drifting dust, a thin spiral of ghostly smoke rising from the dying fire, and the sprawled body of the dead Mexican.

11

POWERS RORKIN drew rein on a serrated hog-backed ridge just after moonrise on the day after the payroll train had been looted. He waited until the others rode up beside him. He pointed down the long, moonlit slopes of blackened rock stippled with thorned brush. "Painted Tanks," he said.

"*Madre de Dios*," said Blas Perez. He shoved up his heavy sombrero and wiped the sweat from his broad forehead. "It is not a moment too soon, *patron*. The water is about all gone."

Far out on the wide sand flats there arose a curious humped formation of light-colored rock. About ten miles beyond the rock formation rose a steeply sloped range of mountains, serving as a vast backdrop to the huge valley. The silvery moonlight gave a mysterious and eerie cast to the stark landscape so that it had a lunarlike quality. There was no sign of human habitation anywhere within that vast shallow bowl where stood the Tanks. There wasn't a trail, road fence, windmill, abandoned *jacal* or a friendly pinpoint of yellow light from some lonely *estancia*.

"Jesus God," said Tod Logan quietly. "Just where are we, Boss?"

"Painted Tanks," said Powers simply. "That's all you have to know right now."

"I have heard of them since I was a boy," said Blas. "To me, they were always just a legend."

"They've been here a long time," said Powers.

"There is water there?" asked the Mexican.

"There better be," said Gil. "We can't ride tomorrow without it. The canteens are dry."

"There will be water there," said his brother. He looked from one to the other of them as he lit a short six. "So far I haven't made any mistakes, have I?"

"Got to hand it to you there, *patron*," said Moss Beckett.

Rorkin blew a casual smoke ring. "We'll hole up there a day or two to rest ourselves and the horses. Then we split. Each pair goes after their cached horses. I've made maps for each of you to show you the shortest way." Rorkin shifted in his saddle. "Logan, you ride back to that last pass. Keep an eye out for pursuit."

"Jesus Christ!" yelled Logan. "Why always me?"

"Everyone else is taking his share of the load. Why not you?" asked Powers.

"Send Cleburne," said Logan.

Powers shook his head. "I need him," he said. He eyed Logan. "You're not thinking by any chance we'll pull out on you, do you?"

"I never said that," said Tod. He wet his dry lips.

"Then do as you're ordered! Go back there. If you see no one is following us, light a small smokeless fire for five minutes on the western slope. I'll have a man on the Tanks to watch for it. If there is pursuit light *two* fires. If there is pursuit and they don't follow into the pass, light *three* small fires. If they go north or south of the eastern mouth of the pass we'll be safe enough until we get out of here. Got it?"

Logan nodded. He was cursing softly as he rode back down the slope.

"He don't like that detail one little bit," said Moss. "He was supposed to ride out of here with Cap Anthony and Cap ain't about to make

212

it now. Tod thinks he's going to be cut out of the loot."

"It's not a bad idea," said Gil. "What about it, Powers?"

Powers touched his tired horse with his spurs. He rode down the slope, and at the bottom he turned. "Spade," he said. "You're the best scout amongst us. Take a *pasear* toward the Tanks."

"That takes time," grumbled Gil. "What the hell is there to worry about, Powers?"

Powers studied the end of his cigar. "Apaches, Lipans, maybe even Quohada Comanches. There isn't any water for thirty miles hereabouts at this time of the year."

"Christ," said Gil. "There won't be nothing but coyotes down there coming for a night drink."

Buck rode past him. "Then you go on down and look, Kid," he said dryly.

"You tryin' to rile me, mister?" snapped Gil.

Buck grinned to himself as he rode down the last of the slope. The long hard ride had taken a lot of starch out of the cocky Kid. Even India Reeves had stood up under the strain better than Gil Rorkin had done.

"I hope a gawd-damned Apache puts a slug

through his head," snarled Gil as he shaped a cigarette.

"He's a good man to have in this *corrida*," said Powers. "He got *you* out of one helluva scrape, and don't forget it!"

"He scouts like an Apache himself," observed Moss Beckett.

"Yeh," said Gil thoughtfully as he lit his cigarette. "Sometimes I do a little wondering about this Spade Cleburne, as he calls himself."

"I don't care if he calls himself Jesus Christ," said his brother. "He's absolutely dependable, which is more than I can say for some in this *corrida*."

Gil angrily jerked the cigarette from his mouth. "You talkin' about me!" he cried.

Powers looked slowly at him. "Shut up, Kid," he said. "I like you much better when your mouth is shut."

Buck dismounted half a mile from the Tanks. He ground-reined his horse and withdrew his Winchester from the saddle scabbard. He levered a round into the chamber. The crisp working of the rifle action sounded inordinately loud in the dreaming, moonlit stillness of the flats. He removed his spurs and padded forward. As he drew closer to the humped rock formation of the Tanks he began to realize how high they really were. They must be thirty-five to forty-feet high on an average. He squatted in the concealing brush and studied them from three-hundred yards away, then encircled the entire formation. There was only one way into the Tanks—a narrow, high-walled passageway like the entrance into the keep of some medieval citadel.

It was deathly quiet. Buck slit his eyes and scanned the moonlit tops of the rock pinnacles. There might be someone up there, lying doggo, with an Indian brown finger pressing gently against a trigger, taking up the slack. His thirst was a brassy corrosion in his throat. It was the thirst that drove him on at last, despite his uneasiness about that silent oval of great rocks sitting out there on the flat desert floor.

He walked softly forward, cocked rifle at hip level, finger pressing in the trigger slack, moving the rifle back and forth in a slow arc, while his eyes probed into every bush and every nook and cranny of those ancient dreaming rocks. He forced himself to walk stealthily into the passageway. A cool draft played about his heated, sunburned face and brought with it the blessed scent of water. He saw the rock tanks, or *tinajas*, five of them, one beside the other, a series of shallow rock pans filled a few inches deep with water that seeped into them from some unknown source deep within the rocks and sands.

The place was empty of human life. He coughed once and the echo came quickly back to him. He dropped to his knees beside the first of the tanks and sipped some of the water. It was gamey, but, by God, it was water. That was all that mattered. If the Tanks had been dry . . . He drove that evil thought from his mind. He walked slowly back through the echoing passageway, shaping a cigarette as he did so. He paused beyond the rocks and looked across the flats to where the thirsty *corrida* and the woman waited tensely for his signal. He looked about him and fully realized the intense loneliness of that almost forgotten place. If Buck Terrell had ever been on his own in his life, facing bitter and almost insurmountable odds, without the slightest hope of help, he was within that position now at Painted Tanks. He lit the cigarette and walked forward, then raised his rifle high in both hands and pumped it up and down three times. In a moment he saw

Powers Rorkin's distant figure ride down the last of the slope toward the Tanks, followed by the others.

12

T HE moon was fully up now, riding serenely in a clear sky, illuminating the desert and mountains almost as though it was daylight. A thread of pale smoke arose from the interior of Painted Tanks, rising straight up into the windless air. Beyond the Tanks the encircling mountains were etched sharply in the moonlight. There was absolutely no sign of life to be seen beyond the Tanks.

Buck Terrell was on first guard atop the great rock wall that encircled the Tanks. From within the interior of the Tanks arose the astringent odor of the burning greasewood, mingled with the stronger odor of coffee. By some acoustic quirk Buck could clearly hear the voices of the others rising from beside the *tinajas*, as they sat around smoking and drinking coffee. India Reeves had been fed and then placed in a shallow cave within the rock wall itself. "Put out that damned fire!" called Buck down into the interior. "That smoke can be seen for miles!"

"Any signal from the pass?" yelled up Powers Rorkin.

"Nada!" yelled back Buck. He shaped a cigarette. He looked toward the distant notch of the pass, hoping to see the twin yellow eyes of two small fires indicating that there was pursuit. It would give Buck a ray of hope. It wouldn't be too long before the *corrida* would scatter to go its separate ways. Powers Rorkin had given no indication of what he planned to do about India Reeves. Buck remembered all too well the Rorkin system—shut mouths permanently. The woman Theresa had been silenced that way, and so had the Mexican Santiago. A cold feeling persisted in creeping through Buck as he thought of it.

Now and then the laughing of Gil Rorkin would drift up to Buck. Buck figured he had a bottle, although the others were not drinking. It was no time to drink, not yet, at least. Drinking didn't seem to have any effect upon the Kid's uncanny speed and accuracy with the twin six-guns.

Buck drew in on his cigarette. It was only a matter of time before Rorkin would make known his decision about India. His eyes caught a faint flareup of light near the pass. He narrowed his eyes. One fire indicated no pursuit. He prayed a little. Moments ticked past. A second fire appeared, like the second yellow eye of a watching cougar. Pursuit! Thank God, thought Buck. He took a drag from the cigarette. Minutes ticked past with the two yellow spots winking faintly at him across the vast sand bowl of the empty valley. He looked down behind him. He opened his mouth to call out to Rorkin. Something made him turn his head. A *third* fire had appeared beside the other two. "Mother of God," he said in Spanish. He remembered all too well what Rorkin had said: "If they go north or south of the eastern mouth of the pass we'll be safe enough until we get out of here."

"You asleep up there, Spade!" yelled Powers.

Buck slowly snuffed out his cigarette butt. He had to answer the man. It wouldn't be too long before Tod Logan would arrive at the Tanks. Buck *had* to answer Rorkin. "Three fires," he said at last.

"Yieeeeee!" yelled Moss Beckett in a real rebel yell.

Gil Rorkin was laughing again, and Buck hated the sound of it as much as he hated Gil Rorkin's guts. In a little while the signal fires were snuffed out one by one and in another half an hour Buck saw a faint trace of dust as Tod Logan spurred on his worn out mount to reach Painted Tanks, for fear the *corrida* might have pulled out on him. No fear of that, thought Buck. They were all there, every damned bloody handed one of them. Powers and Gil Rorkin, Moss Beckett and Blas Perez, as deadly a quartet of killers as one might find in West Texas, with the fifth dusting up a storm to reach them.

Gil Rorkin's voice arose. "Dammit, Powers! I couldn't get her to talk! How'd I know who shot off his mouth to her about the train robbery?"

"Maybe you did it yourself," suggested Moss Beckett.

"You say I did?" demanded Gil.

"I mean, if you was maybe drunk," said Moss.

"I never saw her for months until I walked into the telegraph station!" snapped Gil.

"Cut that out!" said Powers Rorkin. "We've got other more important things to think about now. We hit the train and we got the loot, and we got the girl as well. We've got to think about that loot now. How do we cache it?"

Tod Logan had reached the top of the hog-backed ridge and was slanting down the slope with a thin wraith of dust rising above him in the clear moonlight. The faint drumming sound of the hooves came to Buck. "It's Logan, Boss!" he cried down into the interior of the Tanks.

"We'll wait for Tod," said Powers. "Fill up the cups, Moss."

Buck crawled to the lip of the rocks and looked down on the outlaws. Each of them had his rifle lying beside him. Beyond the ring of outlaws Buck could see the darker mouth of the cave, but he could not see India Reeves. Even as he looked he saw a slender booted foot protrude a little from the cave.

Buck stood up and looked toward the east. Logan was crossing the flats now. In a little while he drew up at the passageway on his lathered horse and flung himself from the saddle. He led the heaving horse in through the passageway, with its hooves echoing loudly up to the place where Buck Terrell stood all alone.

"Here's Logan," said Moss Beckett. He handed the man a cup of coffee. "We're working out the details of the loot," he added.

"I say we split it now!" said Tod.

"Moss?" questioned Powers Rorkin.

Moss looked down at the dying fire. He drained his coffee cup and tossed the dregs atop the ashes, watching the spurt of steam arise. "I think so too," he said quietly.

"Cuchillo?" asked Powers.

Blas shrugged. "I do not think we should come back at all to this part of the country," said the Mexican. "There will be a great price on our heads, and then too, there is the matter of the Texas Rangers. Five of them dead at our hands, *patron*."

"Four!" said Gil.

"You forget the one at Tres Jacales," said Blas.

"It was Cleburne who killed him," said Gil.

Moss spat to one side. "Look," he said. "There ain't one of us who didn't have a hand in killing them Rangers, one way or another. We keep our mouths shut or we all hang together. It was Blas who recognized Francisco Armenderiz and slipped his *cuchillo* into him. It was Gil, as usual, who blew off Armenderiz' face. He's good at that."

"You know what you can do, Beckett," sneered Gil.

223

"It was Tod Logan who found out that Cooke Durkee was a Ranger," continued Moss.

"I useta know him back in the old days," said Tod. He grinned. "By God, he never thought he'd run into his old partner Tod Logan, him being a Texas Ranger and me ridin' with the Rorkin *corrida*. I still think Gil had the right idea in stringin' up Durkee like we had condemned him and executed him. Hawwww!"

Moss lit a cigarette and blew a smoke ring. "I never liked what Gil done to Kelly Ledbetter," he said. "It's one thing to kill a man outright and it's a different matter to finish him off like Gil did."

"It was Blas who stuck the knife into him," said Gil. "Not me."

Blas shrugged. "I did him a favor," he said. He looked at Gil. "The knife is faster than the rope when a man is being dragged to his death behind a running horse."

None of them looked up to see the hat brimmed shadowed face of Buck Terrell looking down on them, nor did they see his big brown hands tighten on the stock and barrel of his Winchester.

Gil glanced at Powers. "It was my big brother

who did himself proud with that kid Ranger," he said a little maliciously.

Powers looked at Gil. He looked down at his hands. "I never killed a man with my bare hands," he said slowly, "until that damned kid came poking about the rancho."

Gil laughed. "Well, the kid didn't have much of a chance when we found out who he was and took away his shiny new guns. By God! That was some riot when the four dogs jumped him! I thought he'd be torn into little pieces!"

Powers did not seem to be listening to his brother. "I broke his damned face with these fists of mine." A strange look crossed his face. His voice rose a little. "I could hear the bones cracking! I never killed a man *that* way before!"

Moss nodded. "You acted just like you was plumb loco," he said thoughtfully.

Powers' expression changed. He plunged his right hand into his coat pocket and threw something onto a flat rock where the moonlight reflected dully from the five objects that lay there. Buck narrowed his eyes. They were Texas Ranger stars. He was sure of it. Four of them reflected the moonlight, but the fifth was blackened. It was the one Powers had taken from the body of the stranger in Tres Jacales.

225

There was something else lying with the five stars—a cheap, coin silver hatband, the one Powers had taken from the sweat stained hat of the Mexican boy he had murdered in the Sierra Vieja. Somewhere within the twisted mind of Powers Rorkin there was evidently a desire to have some memento of the killings in which he had been involved. Powers looked about at the hard faces of his *corrida*. "Those five stars will bind us together in secrecy as long as we ride as a *corrida!*" he said harshly. "If but one of us talks, all of us die by the hangman's rope!"

"You forgot something, *patron*," said Blas. He glanced toward the cave. "The woman," he added.

They all looked toward the cave where India Reeves was held captive. "You'll never keep *her* mouth shut," said Moss. "There's only one way," said Tod Logan. He looked down at his rifle.

"No!" cried out Gil Rorkin. "She's one helluva fine filly! I'll make sure she won't talk! Let *me* have her, Powers!"

Powers relit his cigar. He looked at the faces of his men. "We'll vote on it," he said. "Moss?"

"Get rid of her," said Moss.

"Tod?"

Tod Logan held a thumb down.

"Cuchillo?"

Blas silently drew a brown finger across his throat.

Powers looked at Gil. "Death, as far as I am concerned, Kid," he said.

Gil flushed. He looked wildly about. "What about Cleburne?" he asked.

Powers looked up at Buck. "Spade?" he asked.

Buck grinned. "Yes?" he asked.

"We're voting on the woman," said Powers.

Buck grinned again. "I'll take her any time," he said. "That is, if the Kid isn't man enough to do it."

"God damn you!" snarled the Kid.

"You know what I mean," said Powers to Buck.

Buck had no choice. He was sharply outlined in the clear moonlight. "*Muerte*," he said.

Powers looked about the ring of taut brown faces. "Majority rules," he said.

"Parliamentary procedures," sneered Gil. "Who does the job?"

"Not you," said Moss. "I wouldn't trust my own mother with you, Kid."

227

"What difference does it make now?" asked the Kid.

"We want it clean and final, is all," said Moss. "After all, it is a *woman*."

"Moss is right," said Powers. He reached into a pocket and brought out a deck of cards. He riffled them expertly. "We'll each call for a card. Low man does the job." He placed the shuffled deck on a flat rock. "Cut," he said to Moss Beckett. Moss cut the deck. Powers looked at Tod Logan. "Top card," he said. Tod Logan turned over the top card. "Ace of diamonds," he said. "Never had that kind of luck in poker."

"Moss," said Powers.

Moss wiped his hands on his levis and slowly turned over a card. "Nine of clubs," he said, with a note of relief in his voice.

"Cuchillo," said Powers.

Blas turned over the four of hearts. His hand touched the hilt of his *cuchillo*.

Powers looked at his brother. "You're next, Kid," he said.

Gil's face seemed to fall a little as he turned over the king of spades. The cold-blooded shark *wanted* the job, thought Buck.

Powers looked up at Buck. "You first, Boss,"

said Buck politely. Powers shrugged. He turned over the deuce of diamonds. "Looks like it's me," he said. There was no emotion in his flat voice.

"You can pick for me," said Buck.

Powers shrugged. He turned over the deuce of spades. He looked up at Buck. "It's between you and me, Spade," he said. "Next two cards all right with you or do you want a reshuffle?" They were all looking up at Buck Terrell as he stood there leaning on his grounded Winchester. A thought lanced into Buck's mind. "No need," he said quickly. "I'll do it, Boss."

Powers shook his head. "No," he said. "We'll do it the right way."

Buck hesitated. "All right," he said.

"Ready?" asked Powers.

"Shoot," said Buck.

"My card first," said Powers. He quickly turned over the three of clubs, then looked up at Buck. "You come on down and draw for yourself," he said.

"Too much trouble," said Buck. "Go ahead. Draw for me."

It was very quiet as Powers slowly turned over the next card. Plainly seen in the moonlight was the red four of diamonds. He swept the cards together and evened them off, then thrust them into his pocket. "We'll leave after we divide the loot," he said. "No use in hanging around here. Those men who turned aside at the eastern mouth of the pass might backtrail and come *through* the pass." He looked toward the cave. "There's plenty of time for me to take care of her."

Buck's desperate plan had failed. He had thought if he had won or lost the draw, depending upon how one looked at it, he might have been able to take India out from the Tanks and make a last desperate bid to save her life, hopeless though it seemed. Buck lit a cigarette. Something had made Powers Rorkin change his mind. Originally he had been all for caching the loot and then coming back six months later for it, but *something* had made him change his mind. He could have talked the others into following his original plan. There might be a seed of betrayal sprouting in his devious mind.

The wasteland was bright beneath the moonlight but it was slanting lower in the western sky, casting some shadows within the Tanks. There was not a sign of life out there on the sands. Nothing but the sharply etched shadows of the motionless brush. He could hear Powers

230

Rorkin beginning to count out the loot. There would be six neat piles of fresh bills for each man, about thirteen thousand dollars per man, a neat amount with which to line his wallet. When the moon was down, and India Reeves was stiffening in death, supposedly six men would ride off into the desert, free and clear with their loot and no one to talk about it.

Buck checked his Winchester and Colt, making sure each was fully loaded. He fished out his double-barreled derringer and inserted a pair of fresh .41 caliber cartridges into the chambers. He walked softly back from the inner rim and circled over to just above where India Reeves was located in the cave, waiting for the killing shot of Powers Rorkin. Buck lay belly flat and inched over to where he could just see her below him, seated on a rock with bent head. The shadows had fallen across the interior face of the Tanks wherein was the cave. The *corrida* was moving around beyond the Tanks, saddling their horses.

"India," softly called Buck.

She looked up. He could see her pale face but he could not distinguish her lovely features. "I'll be down to help you in a few minutes," he said.

"Don't be a fool, Buck," she said. "There is nothing you can do to help me now."

"You heard what they plan to do?"

"Yes," she said quietly. "Go away, Buck!"

"I'm coming down," he said. He held his Winchester by the muzzle and lowered it. "Catch my rifle, India." He let go and she caught it deftly. A moment later he hung by his hands and dropped lightly beside her.

"Why die beside me, Buck?" she said. She touched his face with a cool hand.

He looked down at her. "There will be some dying," he promised, "but it might not be the two of us."

"We haven't a chance, Buck!"

He took out his derringer. "I know you can handle this," he said. "Back me up if it gets too hot and heavy for me when the shooting starts."

They could hear the low, muffled voices of the outlaws. Horses were being saddled. Gear was being stuffed into saddlebags. Filled canteens were being hung to saddles. Then suddenly it was very quiet within the great hollow of Painted Tanks. The moon had swung lower. It would soon be time. Rorkin wanted his *corrida* to leave the Tanks when it was dark

232

so that no prying eyes could see them at a distance. Powers Rorkin thought of everything. By the dawn the hard pressed horses would have taken the scattered members of the *corrida* to where the fresh horses had been hidden, waiting for them. By the next day they would be well on their separate ways. In another twenty-four pursuit would be hopeless.

Boots grated harshly on the hard-packed ground beyond the cave. There was a soft rustling of leather and a faint jingling of spurs. Although the moon still lighted the tops of the rock pinnacles the bottom of the interior was now in deep shadows. The movement stopped just beyond the mouth of the cave. The crisp whirring of a revolver cylinder came clearly to India and Buck. Buck bent and kissed the girl, then shoved her behind him. He reached down inside his left boot and fished out his Ranger star and then he pinned it to his shirt front. He wanted all of them now to *know* who he was. On the other hand, he thought grimly, maybe Powers Rorkin would add another star that night to his collection. He picked up his Winchester with his left and then slowly drew and cocked his Colt.

13

THE shadows thickened just beyond the cave. A tall man stood there, his face darkly shadowed beneath his hat brim. A six gun was held at hip level, and the unseen eyes of Powers Rorkin were looking in, seeking the lovely thing he planned to kill in cold blood.

"Rorkin," said Buck softly. He stepped forward.

Powers Rorkin cursed. He jumped back, raising the six gun, but an instant before he pressed the trigger, Buck's Colt flashed and roared deafeningly. The soft slug caught Powers Rorkin just below the heart. The last thing he saw, an instant before he died on his feet, was the scarred face of Buck Terrell and the dull gleaming of the Texas Ranger star on Buck Terrell's shirt front.

Powder smoke drifted upward in the windless air. Buck knelt beside Rorkin and stripped off his coat and hat. He put them on and then pinned the Rangers star to the lapel of the coat, turning over the lapel so that the star could not be seen. Buck swiftly reloaded his Colt and sheathed it. He handed India the dead man's Colt. It was still warm from the hand of Powers Rorkin. She shuddered a little as she felt that warmth.

Buck looked at her. "Ready?" he asked.

"Yes, Buck," she said calmly.

"*Bueno!*" He walked out from the cave into the sheltering shadows. Moss Beckett was filling a large canteen with his back toward Buck. Tod Logan stood by the dying fire, idly kicking sand over it. Blas Perez was tightening his saddle cinch. Gil Rorkin was nowhere in sight. There was no time for Buck Terrell to seek out the fastest gun amongst them.

"About time, Boss," said Beckett over his shoulder. He stoppered his canteen. "You fool around a little bit first?"

"Hawww!" said Tod Logan. His eyes narrowed. "Where'd you get that rifle, Boss? You didn't have one when you went in there."

Buck's Winchester flashed and cracked from hip level. The .44/40 slug smashed into Tod's left arm, inches from his heart. He spun about, sickened by the impact, but he clawed for his Colt with desperate courage. In the instant's time before Logan could draw and fire, Buck crouched and whirled, driving a slug at Moss Beckett. The slug shattered the canteen. Moss cursed as he jumped to one side, dripping with water from the bullet smashed canteen. He drew his six-gun and fired just as Buck dropped to the ground, firing and reloading and firing again in a wild staccato pattern that smashed Moss Beckett into death with half a dozen slugs. Moss fell across the dying fire and lay still.

Buck rolled over and over on the ground as Tod Logan came weaving through the rifted gunsmoke, his broken left arm swinging uselessly and his face twisted with mingled pain and hate. He fired. The slug ripped through the slack of Buck's coat and the next one whipped through the crown of his hat and whipped it from his head.

The rapid gun explosions made a roaring hell of the Tanks and the wreathing smoke gave it semblance of the front porch of Hell itself. Tod Logan dropped to one knee, peering through the smoke. Death came out of that smoke in the insensate shape of a softnosed .44/40 that struck Tod Logan right between the eyes and slammed him flat onto his back where he looked up at the sky with his face a mask of blood.

Buck's Winchester was empty. As he stood

up he hurled the still smoking weapon at the broad face of Blas Perez, who was coming for him through the smoke, six-gun in left hand and deadly *cuchillo* in the right hand. Even as Buck got fully to his feet the Mexican hurled the knife that had given him his nickname of *Cuchillo*. The blade seemed to shimmer dully like quicksilver as it sped toward Buck. He dodged to one side and held up his left arm but the needlelike tip of the blade struck him in the muscular area in front of the left armpit. The excruciating, stunning pain sickened him. He staggered backward. Blas fired his Colt. The slug flicked Buck's right sleeve. He drew and fired from hip level, spinning Blas about. A second slug caught the burly Mexican between the shoulder blades and drove him forward, away from Buck. A third slug hit him low in the back. He turned, with a look of agony on his broad face, pressing his hands against his back. The Colt in Buck's hand seemed like a thing alive, firing and bucking back into the fork of his hand until the hammer clicked on an empty hull. Blas Perez fell backward and lay still beneath the gun smoke, lips drawn back from even white teeth and eyes already glazed in death.

Buck staggered sideways and leaned against the rock wall. He dropped his hot and empty Colt. He was sick and weak with the pain of the knife wound. He gritted his teeth and jerked free the stinging knife tip. He dropped the reddened *cuchillo* and felt an increased flow of blood from the wound.

Buck's sick eyes looked about through the wreathing smoke that seemed to fill the interior of the Tanks. Three men had died in almost as many minutes. Powers Rorkin had gone ahead of the others of his *corrida* to usher their way into Hell. But, *there was something wrong!* Buck passed a hand across his eyes. He looked across the body of Moss Beckett. The mingled smoking stench of burning cloth, leather and singeing human flesh wreathed slowly upward from Moss Beckett. There was a tiny dancing flicker of flame creeping along Moss' vest. The light of the burning cloth grew brighter. It was enough for Buck to see Gil Rorkin. He was standing near the passageway, a cigarette pasted in the corner of his mouth. His hat brim was low pulled, concealing his cold mad eyes. His thumbs were hooked beneath his wide gun belt, just above his twin engraved Colts. The man seemed like a graven statue as he stood there looking at Buck Terrell—the Texas Ranger who had been peddling swift death at Painted Tanks.

Buck looked toward his empty weapons. At any instant Rorkin would draw and fire and Buck knew all too well just how good he was with the six-guns. The bloody knife lay at Buck's feet but he knew better than to try for it, and, in any case, he could hardly get a chance to use it on the Kid.

"I've always wondered about you," said Gil slowly. He walked easily toward the fire with a faint silvery jingling of spurs. He stood there with the stinking smoke rising about his lean and handsome face. "It was my damned fool of a brother who brought you into this *corrida*. The big killer! The fast gun! The wanted outlaw! Spade Cleburne!"

Buck felt the icy sweat of fear work down his sides. The green bile rose a little in the base of his throat. A man doesn't mind dying so much in the heat of fast gunplay, gun against gun, and man against man, but to die like a sheep led to the slaughter is sheer hell on any man, and most particularly a Texas fighting man.

Rorkin rounded the fire and stopped thirty feet from Buck. "You did me a favor at that,"

he said. "Wiped them all out like piss ants."
He grinned. "Leaving ol' Gil with about eighty
thousand dollars and enough fast horses to get
me across the Rio Grande by some time
tomorrow. *Gracias, hombre!*"

"Your brother is dead," said Buck quietly.
He really didn't know *why* he said it to this
cold-gutted shark of a man.

"He was always telling me what to do!"
snapped the Kid.

"You never had the brains or the sense to
think for yourself," said Buck slowly. He was
stalling for time. He knew Rorkin would kill
him and that there was nothing Buck could do
to him physically, but he hated this man with
such a passion he wanted at least to sting that
puffed up ego before he died.

Surprisingly enough, Gil grinned. "Sure," he
agreed. "I haven't the brains to think for
myself. Maybe that's why I stood back and let
you do the job I had been planning all along to
do myself. I could have killed you before you
got Beckett if I had *wanted* to. You damned
fool! Did you think I was missing all the gun
play? Me? Gil Rorkin?"

"I might have known," said Buck.

It was very quiet in the Tanks. The burning

clothing was giving better light and the stench was getting worse.

Gil flipped away his cigarette. He drew out his left Colt and tossed it at Buck's feet. "Pick it up," he said quietly. "Holster it. Don't try to draw yet."

Buck looked down at the fancy Colt. "What do you mean?" he asked.

"You're a fast gun aren't you?" taunted the Kid.

"With a knife hole in me? Losing blood like a stuck pig? I've got a great chance, Kid."

Gil's face worked. "You just killed four men. You want to try for a fifth? A *fast* gun this time, mister!"

Buck's eyes narrowed. In all the time he had known Gil Rorkin and had seen him kill, he had never allowed his victim an even chance against the lightning speed and deadly accuracy of those fancy twin Colts. Something Tod Logan had said the first night Buck had come to the Rorkin rancho now came back to Buck Terrell. "*Makes a difference when a man is up against a fast gun who is willing to kill.*"

"Pick up the Colt," said Gil.

Buck bent and picked up the fancy cutter, with its finely engraved barrel and cylinder, and the ornately carved staghorn grips with their silver mountings.

"Hand honed action by Davis of El Paso," said Gil proudly. "A matched set of Colts, mister. The best in all Texas."

Buck looked at the madman. "How many men have died under these guns, Kid?" he asked.

Gil shrugged. "I don't count Mexes, half-breeds or Indians," he said carelessly.

"*How many men,* Rorkin?"

Gil grinned. "Maybe a dozen."

Buck raised his head. "How many of them had a fighting chance, Kid?" he quietly asked.

Rorkin's eyes narrowed. "What the hell are you talking about? They *all* did! I got a record, mister! There ain't no gun in Texas as fast as mine. Me! Gil Rorkin!"

"You're fast all right, Kid," agreed Buck. He was stalling for time. His right hand itched to drop to that fancy Colt staghorn butt to draw and fire, taking the long chance, but he knew Gil was faster.

The Kid seemed to read Buck's mind. "Draw," he said.

Buck slanted his eyes sideways, hoping to God India would stay quiet until the madman was dead or gone. There wasn't much chance for Buck to leave Painted Tanks alive.

"Draw!" snapped Gil.

Buck slapped his hand down for a draw, whipping the gun out and forward as he thumbed back the big spur hammer, while at the same time he dropped flat on the ground to fire upward an instant after Gil's Colt seemed to leap into his hand and then explode. The slug whipped through the air right where Buck had been standing. Buck's first shot went wide and his second was no better. His vision was a little hazy and he knew that any speed he had once had on the draw was now gone.

Rorkin came forward like a hunting cat to look down at Buck. "You see?" he said triumphantly. "I gave you the bulge and *still* beat you!" His eyes were wide in his head and his breathing was fast and erratic.

There was absolutely no chance for Buck now. He couldn't fire fast enough to hit the man. The cold sweat was running down his body and dewing his face. Fear came to rest on his back and he knew he was going to die.

"The Big Man!" crowed Gil as he moved about, like a cat playing with a mouse. "The Texas Ranger who thought he was too tough

243

and too smart for Gil Rorkin! Well, the others are gone, thanks to you, Cleburne, or whatever the hell your name really is! You know what I am? Me? Gil Rorkin? The Kid?"

Buck looked up at him. "I don't think you know yourself, Rorkin," he said.

"*Ranger Killer!* That's me!"

Buck's hand tightened on the staghorn butt of the fancy Colt. He wanted to shoot. God, how he wanted to shoot!

Something moved softly in the shadows. Buck did not look up at the flushed, triumphant face of the outlaw. Something moved again. The shadows thickened and seemed to grow more substantial thirty feet behind Gil Rorkin. Rorkin cocked his Colt. "You want to die on your feet, Cleburne? Get up! Stand up and face it like a *man*, Ranger!"

India Reeves came out of the shadows with Powers Rorkin's cocked Colt in her small hand. Her right foot struck a stone. The clicking sound alerted Gil. He turned and stared incredulously toward her. "You!" he said in a startled tone. "I thought you were dead!"

She fired at little more than arm's length. The soft .44/40 slug caught Gil in the left shoulder. The slamming impact spun him halfway about.

He went into a crouch and turned back toward her to fire but she fired before he could. The bullet creased the left side of his head. He screamed in anguish as he fired. The bullet went wide. He fired again but India had leapt to one side like a skilled gunfighter. She dropped to one knee and fired upward and then flung herself to one side and fired again. The slamming sound of the shots filled the interior of Painted Tanks. Gil wildly emptied his gun and India fired her last two rounds upward through the swirling, wreathing gun smoke. The slugs drove Gil Rorkin backward against the rock wall of the Tanks. He seemed to hang there for a moment and then he slid downward to sit with his back against the rock wall. Blood mantled his face from the crease wound but his eyes still glared wildly through the mask of blood.

Buck got to his feet and thrust forward his Colt for the last killing shot.

"No, Buck," said India quietly.

He lowered the fancy Colt and she came to him. He put his left arm about her slim waist and felt the weight of her as she grew unsteady on her feet. She stared down at the man to whom she had dealt swift death.

245

Gil closed his eyes. He pawed futilely at the blood running down his handsome face. The whole front of his shirt was soaked with crimson. India Reeves had literally shot him apart, and it was a miracle that he was still alive. He opened his eyes and stared upward at them. "I can't go this way," he said hoarsely. "Not me! Not Gil Rorkin! To die by the hand of a *woman!* Me! Gil Rorkin, the fastest gun in Texas!"

"Be quiet, Rorkin," said Buck quietly. "At least *die* like a man."

There was no response from Gil Rorkin; there never would be again.

India helped Buck to the fire. They dragged the smoldering body of Moss Beckett away from the flames and doused out the burning clothing, but the sickening stench still filled the interior of the Tanks despite the aromatic odor of the greasewood with which India replenished the fire. Buck watched her as she cleansed his knife wound and poured brandy over it. "Waste of good aguardiente," he said dryly.

"Get some sleep," she said quietly. "There is nothing to fear now."

He looked about the interior of the Tanks

and the sprawled and bloody bodies of the dead *corrida*. "No," he said. "Not like this."

She did not argue with him as one by one the horse dragged the stiffening bodies from the interior of the Tanks and dumped them into a cleft below a scaling rock face of the Tanks. He climbed slowly up to the top of the rock wall and dumped and kicked loose scales and pieces of loose rock until the bodies were fully covered. The rock dust drifted off into the dying moonlight. He came down to where she was brewing coffee and cooking a meal. She looked up at him. "You'll need strength to ride, Buck," she said with the great practicality of a woman.

After they had eaten he gathered together the loot from the payroll robbery and stowed it into the Kyacks. He rounded up the horses and lead roped them together. His wound was a dull, aching pain in his shoulder but he would not stay there. She mounted and waited for him as he led his horse through the echoing passageway. The last rays of the dying moon struck a smooth place on the rock wall not far from where the bodies of the Rorkin *corrida* had been buried. Buck looked at the letters that had been carved long ago by some forgotten person who had been there to get water at Painted Tanks. The crude scrawl was in Spanish. "*There is nothing but death here*," read Buck. "Antonio Diaz. May, 1705." He looked at the tumbled rock that covered the Rorkin *corrida*. Even so long ago, Antonio Diaz had carved into the soft rock an accurate prophecy for Painted Tanks and the *corrida* of Powers Rorkin.

They crossed the flat wastes in the very last of the dying moonlight. Buck Terrell looked back just once at the lonely Tanks. Four fine Texas Rangers had died at the hands of those men now lying buried there. The blood debt had been paid off in the same coin by a young woman and a Texas Ranger. *Five Graves to Boot Hill.*

Other titles in the
Linford Western Library:

FARGO: MASSACRE RIVER
by John Benteen

Fargo spurred his horse to the edge of the road. The ambushers up ahead had now blocked the road. Fargo's convoy was a jumble, a perfect target for the insurgents' weapons!

SUNDANCE:
DEATH IN THE LAVA
by John Benteen

The land echoed with the thundering hoofs of Modoc ponies. In minutes they swooped down and captured the wagon train and its cargo of gold. But now the halfbreed they called Sundance was going after it, and he swore nothing would stand in his way.

GUNS OF FURY
by Ernest Haycox

Dane Starr, alias Dan Smith, wanted to close the door on his past and hang up his guns, but people wouldn't let him. Good men wanted him to settle their scores for them. Bad men thought they were faster and itched to prove it. Starr had to keep killing just to stay alive.